SAXBY SMART

PRIVATE DETECTIVE

in

THE TREASURE OF DEAD MAN'S LANE

and Other Case Files

SAXBY SMART

PRIVATE DETECTIVE

in

THE TREASURE OF DEAD MAN'S LANE

and Other Case Files

Simon Cheshire

Pictures by
R. W. Alley

SQUARE
FISH

ROARING BOOK PRESS
NEW YORK

SQUARE
FISH

An Imprint of Macmillan

First published in the U.K. in 2008 by Piccadilly Press Ltd. and
in the United States in 2010 by Roaring Brook Press
First Square Fish Edition: November 2011
Square Fish logo designed by Filomena Tuosto
Book designed by CoolKidsGraphics Inc.
mackids.com

10 9 8 7 6 5 4 3 2 1

AR: 5.1 / LEXILE: 740L

IMPORTANT FACTS

My name is Saxby Smart, and I'm a private detective. I go to St. Egbert's School, my office is in the toolshed, and this is the second book of my case files. Unlike some detectives, I don't have a sidekick, so that part I'm leaving up to you—pay attention, I'll ask questions.

CASE FILE FOUR:

THE TOMB OF DEATH

CHAPTER ONE

I'm not very good at making things. Whenever I put together one of those do-it-yourself models (you know, fighter planes, sports cars, etc.), it always ends up covered in globs of glue. And with a piece stuck on backward. And another piece that falls off as soon as I put the "finished" model on my shelf.

So I should have known better than to try to fix my Thinking Chair. As readers of Volume One of my case files will know, my Thinking Chair is a vital part of my work as a brilliant detective. It's a battered old leather armchair, and in it I sit, and I think, and I mull over important facts regarding whatever case I happen to be working on.

My Thinking Chair had developed a small rip in one of the arms. One afternoon during Spring Break I

was in our toolshed trying to patch it up with a piece of super-tough heavy-duty fix-it tape. *Guaranteed 100% Bonding Power!* it said on the roll. The trouble was, it was 100 percent bonding my fingers together.

Just as I was wishing I'd asked my very practical friend Muddy Whitehouse to do the job for me instead, there was a knock at the shed door. Immediately, I heard the sign fall off (the sign I keep nailing up outside, which says *Saxby Smart—Private Detective*) and sighed.

"Come in!" I called.

In walked Charlie Foster, a boy who's in my grade at school. He's an owlish kid, the kind of person who gives the impression of being chubby even when he's not. He wears tiny round glasses and has a habit of sniffing a lot.

He looked around the cluttered shed. Half of it, as always, was packed with old yard equipment and random tools and things belonging to my dad (I'd found that super-tape in one of his piles). The other half of the shed was crammed with my desk, my files, and my Thinking Chair.

He handed me the sign. "Hi, Saxby. This yours?"

You can tell he's not the
sharpest nail in the toolbox,
can't you? He was looking
a little scared, and holding
a slightly crumpled, handwritten note.

"What can I do for you,
Charlie?" I asked. "Who
told you to come see me?"

He sniffed in amazement.
"How'd you know it wasn't my idea?"

"People who need my services don't usually show
up looking like they don't want to be here," I said.
"Besides, that note you've got there is written in an
adult's handwriting. My guess is that someone's given
you specific information to take along."

"Well, yeah," said Charlie, with another sniff. "My
brother, Ed. He's nineteen."

"And why does your brother, Ed, need my help?"

"His comic was stolen."

My eyes narrowed. "Hm. Yeeees, I can see that that
would be annoying. I don't want to sound rude here,

but, um, wouldn't this be filed under Not That Important? Or maybe, I'll Go Get Another Copy?"

Charlie suddenly seemed to remember the note, and he smoothed it out a little and double-checked some of the writing. "The comic's worth a hundred thousand dollars."

CHAPTER TWO

"How much?" I gasped. "What's it made of, solid gold?"

I fell back into my Thinking Chair. This made the rip even worse, but right then I was only concerned with hearing more about Charlie's problem. Or rather, his brother, Ed's, problem. Charlie blew the dust off an ancient crate of paint cans and sat down.

"Ed collects comics," said Charlie. "He buys and sells them, and he's got shelves full of really old ones, worth a lot."

"Seeing as it's the middle of a weekday, and he's sent you instead of coming himself, I deduce he usually has to be somewhere right now. So trading comics is his hobby, not his job?" I said.

"Yes, that's right," said Charlie. "He works at that

restaurant on Church Street. He's a chef. But he's hoping to trade comics full-time. Or he *was*, until this comic got stolen."

I settled deeper into my Thinking Chair, trying to ignore the low ripping noise coming from its arm. "So . . . Tell me all about this comic, and what exactly has happened."

"It's the first issue of *The Tomb of Death*," said Charlie. He consulted Ed's note again. "Published in 1950. Only a few thousand copies were printed, and there are less than six still known to exist."

"And what's so special about the first issue of *The Tomb of Death*?"

"Dunno, never read it." Charlie shrugged. "But comics collectors dream of owning a copy. It's one of the most valuable comics in the world, Ed says."

"And when was it stolen?" I asked. "Give me every detail you can."

"Ed keeps it . . . er, kept it . . . in our wall safe. Dad had the safe put in because sometimes he keeps a lot of cash in the house, if he can't get to the bank after his store's closed. But Ed uses it the most. *The Tomb of Death* was in a see-through envelope, propped up against the back of the safe."

"And how long had it been there?"

"Ed inherited it a couple of years ago. Our grandfather was really into comics as a kid, and when he died, he left Ed two big boxes of old comics. And one of them was *The Tomb of Death*."

"It was always kept in the safe?"

"Always. Ed hardly ever took it out. It was way too valuable for that, and delicate too. It stayed in the safe twenty-four-seven!"

"Why didn't Ed sell it?"

"I think he was going to. But I'm not sure, you'll have to ask him."

"And when was it stolen?"

"Last weekend. Dad opened the safe on Monday morning, and it was gone."

"Just like that?"

"Just like that."

"Someone cracked the safe? There'd been a break-in?"

"Ed and Dad say no. We have an alarm system, and

it was never triggered. The safe's got an alarm, too, and that didn't go off, either."

"Was it in there on Sunday?"

"Yup. Dad had put his store's weekend earnings in there. The comic was still in the safe then. Definitely. I saw it myself."

"So there'd been a lot of cash in the safe that night?"

"Yeah. That's why the safe was opened up Monday morning—so Dad could take the money to the bank."

Two important clues had already become clear to me. One of them was about the safe, about *how* someone had gained access to the comic. The second important clue was about the comic itself, about *why* the thief had stolen *that*, instead of the money that was there too. Can you work out what I was thinking?

Clue No. 1: If two alarms weren't triggered, and no burglar was involved, then the safe was almost definitely opened by *someone who knew the combination*!

Clue No. 2: If the thief took an old comic but left a pile of cash untouched, then the thief was almost definitely *someone who knew how valuable the comic was.* They knew it was worth more than that pile of cash!

"This is quite puzzling," I mused. "Didn't Ed go to the police?"

"They said there's nothing they can do about it. There wasn't a break-in or anything. It's like the comic just vanished into thin air, overnight."

I stood up decisively. "Okay, these are there two things I'm going to do, in reverse order: No. 2, I'm going to examine the scene of the crime; No. 1, I'm going to try and get this awful super-tough, heavy-duty tape off my fingers. Tell your brother that Saxby Smart is on the case!"

A Page from My Notebook

QUESTION: If the comic was so valuable, why did Ed keep it? Why not sell it and use the money to set himself up as a full-time comics trader, which is what Charlie said he wants to be?

QUESTION: What kind of thief would steal a comic, but not money? Even if a thief saw a comic in a safe and thought, "Aha! I bet that's worth a lot," surely he'd have taken the money too. Why was this thief <u>only</u> interested in the comic? This is definitely significant.

QUESTION: Will I be scraping these gluey chunks off my hands for the rest of time?

CHAPTER THREE

First thing the next morning, I took a bus to Charlie's house. As I rumbled through town, I called my super-brainy friend and all-around research genius, Isobel "Izzy" Moustique.

"How much?" she gasped.

"That's exactly what I said," I told her. "I'm on my way to the scene of the crime right now."

"A comic book that rare and valuable would be really hard to sell without attracting attention," said Izzy. "This must be a pretty stupid thief! There's no way they could do *anything* with that comic without getting noticed."

I shrugged. "They could read it."

"What? You're telling me a comic like that wouldn't have been reprinted and republished in a dozen different books by now? No, nobody would steal it just to see what was inside."

"I guess not," I said, trying to sound as unembarrassed as possible. "Anyway, think you could see what you can come up with? Information on recent sales of rare comics, that kind of thing?"

"Already on it," said Izzy. "Come and see me later."

As the bus chugged and bumped along the town's main shopping streets, something struck me about what Izzy had said. She was right—the thief would find it almost impossible to sell that comic without getting noticed.

Unless . . .

Unless they didn't plan to sell it at all. Suddenly, I jumped up with a cry! It startled the old lady in the seat behind me.

"Have you missed your stop, sweetie?" she asked.

"No, I've missed an obvious suspect!"

She gave me a funny look. I think she thought I was a little nuts.

But there *was* an obvious conclusion to be drawn here. What sort of person would steal that comic book and not intend to sell it? Only one sort of person, as far as I could see! Can you see it too?

Another *collector*, like Ed! Someone who might want to keep the comic just for its rarity alone.

At last the bus reached my stop. The old lady clutched her shopping bag and watched me nervously as I raced to get off. I hurried over to Charlie's house. He took me up to Ed's room first, so I could finally meet his brother.

They say that the clothes you wear say something about you. If that's true, then the clothes Ed wore said something rather obnoxious. With a hand gesture added in for punctuation. He was, without a doubt, the scruffiest person I'd ever seen in my life. He looked like he'd found his T-shirt and jeans in a Dumpster, and he had a patchy beard that reminded me of chocolate sprinkles on ice cream. Apart from all that, he was simply a larger version of Charlie.

His room, tucked away in a converted attic at the top of the house, was his exact opposite. It was amazingly neat and clean. An entire wall was covered in white bookshelves, and placed on those shelves were hundreds—no, thousands—of plastic envelopes. Just visible inside each envelope was the outer edge of a comic book, and most of the envelopes had hand-

written labels attached to them.

Ed was sitting in front of his computer. As soon as Charlie and I came in, he bounded over to me and shook my hand so enthusiastically I thought my teeth would come loose.

"Hi!" he said. "You must be Saxby. Charlie's told me all about your exploits, kid. I hope you're as good as they say you are."

"Better!" I declared with a grin. "Now then, tell me more about this comic."

Over some milk and fancy chocolate cookies ("Ooh, yes, I'll have another one of those," I said. "Thanks!"), Ed told us the tale of *The Tomb of Death* with a wild gleam of excitement in his eyes.

"Way back in the 1950s," he said, "*The Tomb of Death* was the first in a new style of comic books. Full of grisly stories about murder plots, evil curses, and horrible monsters. These comics were a hit. Kids

17

loved them. And within a couple of years, they were banned!"

"Banned?" I said. "Were they really that bad?"

"Nah," said Ed. "They were funny! With a few scares thrown in, of course. The thing is, parents started saying they were a bad influence on children, and they were banned: *The Tomb of Death*, *The Valley of Slime*, all of 'em."

"I see," I said. "They weren't published for long, and parents would get rid of them wherever they could. Result: they end up collector's items."

"Precisely!" cried Ed. "There are certain comics that are legends in the world of collecting. Like, for instance, the *Action Comics* issue from the 1930s, when Superman first appears, or Batman's arrival in *Detective Comics* a little later. Or Issue Number 15 of Marvel's *Amazing Fantasy*—that's the origin of Spider-Man; that comic's worth a fortune."

"And *The Tomb of Death* is as famous as those?"

"Wellllll," said Ed, making a face and rocking his head from side to side. "It's less sought after, but it's so unusual, it's worth at least as much."

My earlier thoughts about another collector being the thief sprang to mind. "Did you keep the comic a secret? Did other collectors know you had it?"

"Of course they knew!" cried Ed. "I mean, what's the point of having the first issue of *The Tomb of Death* in your collection if you don't tell the world?"

"You weren't worried one of them might try to steal it?"

"To be honest, no," said Ed. "It was in that safe, locked away."

"And it never came out of the safe?"

"Never. Well, except for special occasions, and even then it never left my sight."

"What sort of special occasions are we talking about here?"

"Uh, lemme see . . . " said Ed, wrinkling his nose in thought. "*American Comics* magazine did an article on my collection about a year ago. They took a picture of me holding up the comic. Then I took it to a trade show soon after that."

"What's a trade show?" I asked.

"Basically, a comics convention," said Ed. "Lots of

traders, lots of buying and selling going on, comics publishers showing off their latest stuff, that kind of thing."

"An ideal opportunity for a thief!"

Ed shook his head. "That comic was in a sealed, see-through envelope that never left my hands. I even took it to the bathroom with me! It was perfectly okay."

"Was that the last time the comic was taken out of the safe?"

"No, there was one more time, about four months ago. I took it out to show Rippa. He's another collector. He's got a shop in town, directly across from the restaurant I work at. That's how I got to know him. Odd fella. Not really someone you'd trust."

"I see," I said quietly.

Ed could see what I was thinking. "I can see what you're thinking," he said. "No, he never even touched it. Anyway, you shouldn't ever touch comic books that old."

"Not touch them? Why?"

"They were printed on really cheap paper. High acid content in the wood pulp that was used to make it, you see, so after a few years the paper literally starts to crumble. That's another reason why certain comics are so rare. Most copies have simply fallen apart. You've got to keep the air off them, and keep 'em away from sunlight. Like vampires." He pointed to the neatly stacked comics on his shelves. "Why else do you think I keep all those in plastic sleeves?"

"So this Rippa didn't even touch it?"

"Nope. I did take the comic out, though, and turned the pages so we could both admire the thing. Wonderful smell comes off them, you know, the smell of history. Of course, I wore cotton gloves. Even the tiny layer of sweat on your fingertips can damage the paper."

All this time, Charlie was being oddly quiet. He kept sipping his drink and staring at the rows and rows of sealed-up comics.

"So," I said, "if the rest of the collection is kept up here, instead of in the safe, I assume none of these are anywhere near as valuable?"

"Correct," said Ed. "But there's some really interesting stuff here. Take this one, for instance . . . "

Ed Foster might have dressed like a walking trash can, but he was clearly an expert on the history of comic books.

He explained to me why some issues were more collectable than others (Issue 33 of *The Amazing Spider-Man*, for example, worth more than Issues 32 or 34 because it contains a really well-known story. Or Issues 12 to 22 of *The Purple Avenger*, worth just fifty cents each because the artwork was garbage. Fascinating stuff!). By the time Ed had given me his eager guided tour of the shelves, I was ready to rush out and start a collection of my own!

Charlie kept peeking over his brother's shoulder, trying to get a look at whatever Ed was showing me. Drips from his almost-empty glass plopped onto the carpet.

"Hey, Charlie!" cried Ed. "Watch it! You get any of that on these comics, and you're in for it! You know you're barred from the whole collection."

"Barred?" I said.

"Yeah," said Ed, eyeing his brother moodily. "Ever since I let him borrow one of my 1960s *Fantastic Four*s and he got jelly all over it."

Charlie stuck his tongue out at Ed. (Actually, no, he didn't do that. Actually, he said a short sentence which included the words "complete" and "you," and which I shouldn't repeat here!)

"Can I see the crime scene now?" I said quickly.

We went downstairs. The safe was recessed in the wall of the living room and concealed behind a painting that swung out on hinges like a door. The rest of the room was just an ordinary living room: sofa, a couple of chairs, TV in the corner.

The safe had a standard combination lock, a big dial in the middle of the door that you turned back and forth to line up with a series of numbers. Ed opened it, standing close to the dial so that nobody could get the combination by watching him. All that was inside was a small pile of papers.

"That's all Dad's," said Ed. "Stuff about the house, insurance, and so on."

"And the comic was propped up at the back there?"

"Yup."

"In full view, so you'd know right away it was gone?"

"Yup."

"No way it could slip out of sight, or get mixed up with those papers?"

"Nope."

I remembered my earlier deduction, put forth in Chapter Two: if the safe hadn't been broken into, then the thief had to be someone who knew the combination.

I asked Ed where the combination was kept. He tapped the side of his head. "In here," he said. "There's only me, Mom, and Dad who know it. None of us have it written down. None of us have ever told anyone else what it is."

"*I* don't know the combination," said Charlie. "They won't even tell me what it is. I've never opened that safe in my whole life."

At that point, I have to admit I was out of ideas. The theft of the comic book seemed almost impossible. So only those three people could have opened the safe?

Suddenly, I wasn't out of ideas anymore! If the thief didn't *break into* the safe, and the thief couldn't *open* the safe (assuming, of course, that neither Ed nor his parents were the thief!), then there could be one—and only one—way the thief could have struck.

Can you see what it is?

25

The thief could only have struck when the safe was *already open*.

"This Rippa guy," I said. "Was he here in the room when you opened the safe to show him the comic?"

"Yeah," said Ed.

"Aha!" I cried.

Ed waved his hands around. "Hang on, hang on! I wondered about that too. But the comic was here when he left. Under lock and key, back in the safe. I put it there myself."

"Was Rippa left alone with the comic?" I asked.

"Only for a couple of minutes," said Ed. "I'd just finished showing him the pages. I'd put it back in its case, and the doorbell rang. As soon as I came back into the room, I realized what I'd done—I'd left the comic unattended! But Rippa was sitting over there, flipping through some magazines he'd brought along. The comic was untouched. Safe in its case. He had *not* stolen it."

I sat on the sofa. "Hmm, yes. You'd have to be a pretty stupid and desperate thief to try to snatch that comic right up from under your nose."

"Exactly," said Ed. "Even if he'd *thought* about stealing it, he couldn't possibly have *done* it."

"Hmm," I said again. "Well, *someone* 'done it.'"

I thanked Ed for the milk, took another chocolate cookie for the journey home ("Ooh, thanks, don't mind if I do!"), and headed for the bus stop.

Once I was back in my shed, I sank into my Thinking Chair to mull over the facts. Then I stood up, pulled a piece of that wretched super-tough, heavy-duty tape off the back of my pants, and sank into my Thinking Chair again.

PROBLEM: Logic says, "You'd steal that comic in order to sell it." But! Nobody could ever sell it without being noticed.

PROBLEM: Logic says, "The person who wouldn't steal it to sell it would be another collector." But! As Ed explained, half the point of having a rare comic in your collection is to show it off. The thief would never be able to do that without arousing suspicion. (In fact, they'd have to go to great lengths to stop anyone from knowing they have it!)

PROBLEM: Logic says, "Either the thief opened the safe, or the thief struck when the safe was open." But! Both those options now seem to be ruled out. Unless...

QUESTION: Could Ed have done it himself, for some unknown reason? Or, could his mom and dad have done it, for some equally unknown reason? Must investigate further!

FACT: Charlie is barred from looking at Ed's entire collection. Which seems a little mean, but I guess I can understand it. I'd bar Charlie from my shed if he started getting jelly on my case files!

FACT: The rip in my Thinking Chair is getting worse. Must remember to call Muddy.

CHAPTER FOUR

The sign over the shop said *Comix Nirvana* in big bubbly letters, with *We Buy, Sell, X-change* in smaller bubbly letters underneath. Below the sign, on a handwritten sheet taped to the store window, was *No Time Wasters!* (I assumed this meant "serious collectors only," rather than being some sort of sci-fi warning that they were out of stock of something called *Time Wasters*. But I couldn't be sure.)

The store was tucked away at the far end of Church Street, just outside the center of town. Across from it, and about a quarter mile up the road, was La Pizzeria, the restaurant where Ed Foster worked as a chef.

As soon as I entered Comix Nirvana, I got the distinct feeling I was being watched. And I don't mean that they had security cameras. Behind the counter, perched on a high stool and flipping through a gaming magazine, was Rippa. His beady eyes followed me as I strolled around the store, pretending to browse but keeping an eye out for clues.

It was a small shop, no bigger than my classroom. Shelves of action-packed covers stretched from floor to ceiling, right around the walls. The ceiling itself was papered over with old movie posters, announcing that *It Came from Space* and *The Astro-Zombies Have Arrived*. Beside the counter was a huge wooden display case raised up on thick legs, divided into sections. Inside each section were some of the same kinds of plastic sleeves that Ed used, containing comics with covers that were slightly wrinkled and faded.

"These are your old comics?" I asked innocently. "The really collectible ones?"

Rippa nodded. He seemed to be in his early twenties, was thin with gelled-back hair, and wore a creased white collared shirt with a loosely knotted tie. Ed had told me that his real name was Tarquin, and that anyone who called him Tarquin had something thrown at them.

"You buying?" he said.

"Yes, I might be," I said brightly. "My sweet old grandma has given me a huge wad of birthday cash, and I thought I'd invest in some vintage comics."

"Wise move," said Rippa with a smile that made me think of cold gravy. (I *really* don't like cold gravy.)

My mission at Comix Nirvana was twofold: 1) to observe Rippa in his
natural habitat, and 2) to see what useful information I could gather. My investigations would hit a dead end, and fast, if I couldn't establish more facts about the suspects.

"Anything in particular you looking for?" said Rippa. He pointed to the wooden box. "Lots of rare items in there."

The shelves around the walls were crammed, overflowing even, but this case had plenty of space in it. I wasn't sure what that might mean: had there been a sudden craze for vintage comics? Or was Rippa simply not that good at keeping old issues in stock? I casually leafed through the case.

"How about those *Purple Avenger*s there?" said Rippa. "I've got every one from Issue 10 to 25. Worth twenty-five bucks each because of their age, but I can let you have them for twenty apiece."

"Mmm, no," I said, alert as ever. "I'm not really a *Purple Avenger* fan." (This was perfectly true—for more on this, see my earlier case file, *The Mark of the Purple Homework*!)

"See that one there?" asked Rippa. "That's it, the issue of *Mars Robot Rampage*. You can take it out of its sleeve and have a look if you like. Printed in 1938, that was. Nobody's got a complete set of those, not anywhere in the world. I've got only the one issue, so I'm selling it cheap—just sixty dollars."

I took out the comic and flipped through it. Giant machines with laser guns for eyes zapped up at me from the smooth, brightly printed pages.

Destroy All Earthlings!; *Run, Penelope—we don't stand a chance!*

That settled it. This short conversation had given me *proof* that Rippa was a crook, or at least that he was willing to rip off his customers. In fact, I now had two very specific examples of how happy Rippa was to engage in some shady dealings.

Thinking back on my meeting with Ed Foster, can you deduce what these two examples were?

Proof #1: Those issues of *The Purple Avenger* weren't worth anything like twenty dollars each, as Ed had explained to me.

Proof #2: If that issue of *Mars Robot Rampage* really *was* printed in 1938, it should have been in a very delicate, crumbling state. No collector would ever let someone handle it so casually! Rippa was clearly lying about its age.

"Mmm, I think I'll leave it for now," I said.

"Don't leave it for long," said Rippa. "You won't get offers like that from other dealers."

"That's very true," I said, nodding wisely.

I headed for the street, but then paused with the door ajar. "By the way," I said, "do you have the latest issue of *Time Wasters*?"

"What?" grunted Rippa. "No, I don't! Can't you see the sign in the window?"

CHAPTER FIVE

I went to see Izzy, Queen of All Info. Her room was looking particularly fluffy, sparkly, and other girly adjectives. The chunky rings on her fingers caught the light from the disco ball attached to the ceiling.

She set her laptop to Sleep and spun around in her swivel chair to face me. She consulted a stack of printouts to recheck her facts.

"Okay, two things," she said. "First, this Rippa character is perfectly willing to get involved in some shady dealings."

"Yes, I've noticed that too," I said. "What did you find out?"

"A couple of years ago he was caught trying to pass off a facsimile edition as the real thing."

"A simmy-what?" I said.

"A facsimile," said Izzy. "Now and then, comics companies will republish a particularly famous or popular old comic. Same interiors, same cover, and so on. These facsimile editions are just casual collectors' items really, to give you the look and feel of an old comic without actually having to fork over the money for the real thing."

"That sounds a little sneaky," I said, wrinkling my nose.

"Oh, there's nothing crooked about it," said Izzy. "These facsimiles are clearly sold as 'not the real thing.' They're very popular with comics fans."

"And Rippa tried to sell one as though it were old and valuable."

"Right," said Izzy. "If you know nothing about comics, it's juuust possible that someone like Rippa could fool you into thinking you were buying the real thing. Anyway, he got found out at the last minute. He claimed it was a mistake. Which, to be fair, it might have been. But there are some dealers who still won't trade with him."

"Hmm," I pondered. "Too bad Ed Foster isn't one of them. Anything else on Rippa?"

"I checked the auction Web sites; there are several specific trading sites where comics dealers do business. One thing's for sure: Rippa has never sold, or bought, a single copy of *The Tomb of Death*. Not any issue, not ever."

"That's definite?"

"Absolutely. And by the way, his real name is—"

"Tarquin, yes, I know. I've been trying to think of a way to see if he really does throw something at you if you call him that."

Izzy dropped her pile of printouts back on her desk. "You know, Saxby, I think you're barking up the wrong tree with Rippa. Considering the scene of the crime, and what happened, I don't see how he could possibly have stolen that comic. Besides, he knows he's got a bad reputation, he knows he'd be Suspect Number One in a case like this. He'd be a fool to try something."

"I dunno," I muttered. I suddenly remembered that wooden display case in Rippa's shop. I'd wondered why it seemed half empty. And now, a specific question came to mind: "Has Rippa been selling off a lot of his stock lately?"

Izzy flipped back through her printouts. "He's sold tons of stuff in the past couple of months, yes. And by the looks of it, he hasn't bought very much."

"Hmm . . ."

"I still think there are better suspects out there," said Izzy. "What about Ed's dad, for example? He had easy access to the safe."

I snapped my fingers. "Aha! He owns a store! He could be in debt . . . he could have all *kinds* of money problems!"

"I'm way ahead of you," said Izzy quietly, with a smug smile, picking out a page from the pile of her printouts. "I've already checked."

"Aha!" I cried. "What a fool I was, not to notice it at once! Ed's dad is in financial trouble! He sees the comic in the safe! He spots a way to clear his debt! He takes the comic! He sells it! Suddenly, his money worries are over! Am I right? Am I right?!"

"No."

"Oh."

"His dad's store is doing really well, actually. Has been for years."

"Oh. Another theory blown out of the water, then . . . "

"Looks like it," said Izzy, doing a slow spin in her swivel chair. "But I still think Ed's dad is a more likely suspect than Rippa. Face it, Saxby—this might just be the case that beats you."

She eyed me with a sly smile.

"Never," I said, eyeing her without so much as a hint of a sly smile. "Nobody gets the better of Saxby Smart."

FACT: If Rippa _does_ have the stolen comic, he certainly isn't trying to sell it.

QUESTION: Did he steal it just to keep it? Possibly, but Izzy says he's never bought or sold any issues of The Tomb of Death, ever. Which implies that he's not actually a fan of the series. So why steal it to keep it?

FACT: Rippa's been selling a lot of other comics lately, but he's not been buying much.

QUESTION: Why? Does he need money for something? If so, _what_?

QUESTION: Is Izzy right? Does Ed's dad have something to do with this, something I haven't spotted yet?

PROBLEM: If Ed's dad _is_ involved, I'm going to be stirring up all kinds of trouble—Ed and Charlie won't be happy to discover the thief's identity!

PROBLEM: What am I going to do about my Thinking Chair? That rip is getting worse. And I'm not even going _near_ that tape again!

CHAPTER SIX

The next day at school, the case took a decisive turn. And a very unexpected turn it was too!

For most of the morning, I found it hard to concentrate in class. Which is normal when we're doing math, because Math is certainly not my best subject. But today, I was finding it particularly hard to concentrate because of the problems surrounding that comic book. The crime *seemed* impossible, and yet it had happened. The suspects *seemed* in the clear, and yet someone must have—

"Saxby Smart?" called Mrs. Penzler, our home room teacher.

"Er, sorry?" I blinked.

"Are you with us today, Saxby?" snapped Mrs.

Penzler. The rest of the class giggled. Even Muddy! I glared at him, and he gave me a big, cheesy grin.

"Give us the answer to question three, Saxby!" cried Mrs. Penzler.

I hadn't the faintest idea what she was talking about. However, Mrs. Penzler is a no-nonsense teacher, and she likes definite answers, so I gave her the most definite answer that popped in my head.

"Fourteen," I said. Definitely.

"It's two-point-two," said Mrs. Penzler, with a bemused look on her face. "See me afterward, and I'll go over this topic with you. Again."

I sighed and settled down to untangling the jumble of numbers on the page in front of me. I tried hard to follow the rest of the math lesson, but to be honest, I found it about as easy as eating ice cream with chopsticks. My spirits perked up when the bell for lunch went off, and then they slumped back down again when I remembered my after-class appointment with Mrs. Penzler. Our ten-minute chat had two very important results, however.

Result No. 1: "Oh, I seeeee!" I finally got what

she'd been going on about during the whole class. It was as if the chopsticks had been replaced with a spoon!

Result No. 2: It made me late for lunch. Which made me late for what I had to do after lunch (namely, helping to put up an art display outside the school office). Which meant I was standing outside the school office when Charlie Foster turned up. If I hadn't been late, I'd have missed him entirely.

He was carrying his schoolbag, and clearly hadn't expected to see me. He gave me a kind of nervous nod and a "Hello" and went into the office, where he was out of sight and out of earshot.

The display was just about finished. The two other kids on display duty went back to their classrooms, leaving me to pin up the last couple of labels (*A Map of the Town by 4B* and *By Timmy Liggins of 2L—Miss Bennett says, "Lovely work, Timmy, well done."* I mean, ick!).

A few seconds after Charlie had entered the office, Mrs. McEwan, the school secretary hurried out. She click-clunked on her tottering high heels over to the teachers' lounge, her whole body swaying back and forth on her chunky bare legs.

Kids weren't normally allowed in the school office on their own. It occurred to me that Charlie had told her about some terribly urgent problem to get her out of the way. I stepped out of sight, behind the display boards. Something was going on.

From inside the office came a loud whirring noise. Then Charlie emerged, still carrying his bag. He had a look about him that could only be described as gleeful. Something in that office had made him very happy indeed.

As soon as he'd gone, I emerged from my hiding place and sneaked into the office myself. If I was found in here without good reason, I could be in big trouble. I needed to identify what Charlie had been doing, and fast.

Suddenly, I heard the click-clunk of those high heels, heading back this way! I had time to look in one place only, and I had a choice of:

- Mrs. McEwan's desk and the heaps of stuff on top of it.
- The trash can beneath the desk.
- The cupboard under the window.
- The big paper shredder beside the cupboard.
- A box of just-delivered stationery.
- The office computer perched on its rolling cart.

The choice was actually quite simple. Have you spotted it?

I went straight to the paper shredder. What else would have made that loud whirring noise I'd heard? (Well, unless Charlie had suddenly started doing machinery impressions in his spare time . . . or the computer needed some serious repairs . . .)

"Charlie Foster, you insolent child!" cried Mrs. McEwan, clattering back into the room. "Mrs. Penzler does not need an emergency box of paper clips, and—"

She stared at me. I think, just for a second, she thought Charlie had suddenly mutated into a different kid.

"I've been sent to empty the shredder," I lied quickly, unhooking the big plastic trash bag beneath the machine.

"Oh," said Mrs. McEwan. "Thank you. If you see Charlie Foster, tell him he's an insolent child."

"I will," I said, dragging the bag out of the office.

I took the bag over to the recycling bin outside the teachers' lounge. I carefully opened it up and peered inside. Most of the shreds were plain white strips of paper, but sitting among them were thin slices of something else. I picked up a handful.

These shreds were a brownish-white, with multicolored parts. The paper felt thin and soft between my fingers. I lifted one to my nose. There was a dusty smell, a smell I'd smelled once before. With a sudden feeling in my stomach as if it had been tied to a giant boulder and thrown off a cliff, I realized what Charlie had been doing.

Have you figured it out too?

He'd just shredded *The Tomb of Death*.

I gasped. Loud. I collapsed. Onto the floor. Charlie Foster had just shredded a comic book worth . . . I gasped again.

So *Charlie* had stolen the comic? I could hardly believe it. A dozen enormous questions suddenly popped into my head, most of them beginning with "Wait a sec, how on earth . . . ?"

Mrs. Penzler emerged from the teachers' lounge and loomed over me. "If you're emptying that bag, then get it emptied and run along to class. Honestly, Saxby, you're in a world of your own today!"

I pulled the remains of the comic out of the bag and stuffed them into my pockets.

There had to be more to this than I was seeing. There just *had* to be. As soon as school was over, I hurried home to my Thinking Chair. Sitting down carefully so that I didn't make the rip on the arm any worse, I settled down with my notebook, my sharpest pencil, and my brain cells.

PROBLEM: Okay, assuming Charlie is the thief, he must have opened the safe. Which means he must have known the combination. How?

FACT: Only Ed and his parents know the combination. They say they've never told anyone what it is. And even if they _had_ told Charlie, they'd have no reason to hide that fact.

CONCLUSION: Charlie _found out_ the combination.

QUESTION: How? Certainly not by sneakily watching someone—Ed made it clear that angle was covered!

PROBLEM: Sure, Charlie would get in big trouble for stealing the comic. But why _destroy_ it? An incredibly valuable thing like that? He'd be in _much_ more trouble for destroying it. Something about this simply _does not add up_.

CHAPTER SEVEN

The following day (Saturday), I asked two specific questions. The answers to those two questions finally gave me the key to the entire case.

The first question was one I asked Izzy. I called her up and said: "Safes. Like the one the Fosters have. Can you set your own combination for them, or do they come with one that you can't change?"

Ten minutes later, she called me back. "Most of them have a user-set combination. You can use whatever numbers you like. People usually choose something memorable, like a birthday or their house number."

Aha!

The second question came a little later. This time, I called Ed Foster. I said, "I have something here I'd like you to look at."

He said, "No problem, I'll come over right away."

Twenty minutes later, a dilapidated, banged up car chugged and shuddered onto the small paved driveway in front of my house. I suppose it makes sense that a guy as scruffy as Ed Foster would have a seriously trashed car like that. Owner and vehicle in perfect harmony.

Unfortunately, Ed had brought Charlie along. I'd been hoping he wouldn't, but it was too late now. I'd just have to risk it.

This whole meeting was a risk. I needed to show Ed some of the shredded remains of the comic. I was hoping he wouldn't realize exactly what it was I was showing him.

Ed and Charlie came out to my shed. I took just two of the shreds out of my filing cabinet, as Ed sat perched on my desk. The minute Charlie saw them, he started to shuffle nervously. He realized at once that I must have followed him into the school office. I tried not to give away the fact that I knew that he knew that I knew what those shreds were. I told myself to play it cool.

So now, here comes that vital second question:

"What can you tell me about these?" I asked Ed, handing him the two shreds.

He frowned, then raised his eyebrows. "Well, they're shredded paper," he said.

My heart was thumping. I needed to establish the age of these shreds. It was central to the whole case. I also needed to choose my words very, very carefully, or I'd have a babbling wreck of a comics collector on my hands. "I mean, can you tell me anything about the paper? I only ask because you know a lot about whether or not some types of paper are old or new."

Ed examined the shreds closely, turning to hold them up to the light coming through the Plexiglas window. "Well, this could be standard comic book stock," he said at last. "You see the way the colored ink there is printed in tiny dots? That's certainly what you'd see in older comics."

I glanced over at Charlie. He'd gone as pale as a ghost in a snowstorm.

"So . . . the paper . . . itself . . . " I said.

"Oh, that's not old," he said confidently.

I snapped to attention. "It's not? That's *not* from a really old comic book?"

"No way," said Ed. "What on earth made you think so? No, if you put old pulp paper through a modern shredder, you'd end up with a bunch of little pieces, not neat shreds like this. I told you, that old paper is really delicate."

Aha Number Two!

And it wasn't the "aha" I'd been expecting. The age of that paper was indeed central to the whole case, but in a way I hadn't quite foreseen. Suddenly, the theories I'd been working on in my head needed to be reversed.

"That's it!" I declared. "I've solved the case!"

"Really?" cried Ed, grinning. "So where's my comic book?"

Charlie had turned almost see-through, he was so pale. If he hadn't been leaning on the lawnmower off in the corner, I think he'd have fallen over.

"I'll explain everything when we get to Rippa's store," I said.

"It's closed today," said Ed.

"Why?"

"He's going to L.A."

"Why?"

"The International Comics Convention," said Ed. "It starts tomorrow."

Now it was my turn to go pale. I leaned against my Thinking Chair to stop myself from falling over.

"Of course," I gasped. "*That's* what he's been saving up for."

"Sure, it's an expensive trip," shrugged Ed. "Are you telling me *he's* got my comic?"

I nodded. Charlie stared at me, open-mouthed with relief.

"Right!" declared Ed. "When he gets back, I'll—"

"No, you don't understand!" I cried. "We have to stop him from going, or you'll never see that comic again!"

"Impossible," Ed wailed. "If his flight hasn't already left, it's going to go real soon."

"What about your car?" I said. "It's only twenty miles from here to the airport."

"Impossible," Ed wailed. "The radiator's busted.

It's got a leak. That car's got a range of about three miles, at most. How about the bus? Or a taxi?"

"Too slow," I said. "We need to get there now!"

Charlie slid to the floor with a bump. "That's it, then," he said mournfully. "It's gone. Rippa's won."

Ed let out a yelp of anger and panic. I looked around quickly. There had to be something we could do. There had to be some way to fix that car.

And as I looked around my shed, an idea struck me. There was something here that had been giving me no end of trouble, but which might, just, make a temporary seal for the car's radiator.

Think back . . .

"Look!" I cried, snatching up the roll of super-tough heavy-duty tape I'd been trying to use on my Thinking Chair. *"Guaranteed 100% Bonding Power!"*

Ed took the roll from me. "Brilliant."

The three of us raced out to the car. Ed hurriedly taped up the leak and refilled the car's radiator from the plastic water bottle he had in the trunk.

"So, Saxby," said Charlie quietly. "How exactly did Rippa steal the comic?"

Ed jumped into the driver's seat. "Yeah!" he cried. "I wanna know too!"

"I'll explain on the way," I said. "Now *move!*"

We buckled up as Ed shifted the car into reverse, and it lurched around in a semicircle. With tires screeching like a fast getaway car in a movie, the vehicle bounded for the street.

"Well?" said Ed, as he drove around a sharp bend and headed for the side road that fed into the high-way.

"Well," I said, watching the median strip zip past at a frightening speed and wishing I hadn't been quite so insistent on getting there as fast as possible, "the thing is, what took me ages to realize is that there were two thefts here, not one."

"Two?" said Ed, maneuvering the car onto the highway and revving up to just below the speed limit.

"Yes," I said. "The first happened because the thief saw a chance and took it. The second was carefully planned. Okay, let's consider the second one first. Ed, do you have a firm hold of that steering wheel?"

"Yeah, why?" said Ed.

"Because I've got to tell you that the second crime was done by Charlie."

"*What?!*" yelled Ed. He whizzed the car into the fast lane, and we were all thrown from side to side. Charlie buried his face in his hands.

"Charlie Foster, you thieving little twerp, I'll—" cried Ed.

"Shut up!" I cried. "You just concentrate on driving! Yes, Charlie did it, but hear me out. He didn't mean any harm. He only wanted to borrow the comic for a bit. Am I right, Charlie?"

"Yes," mumbled Charlie from behind his hands. "I'm sorry, Ed, really. I wish I'd never even heard of that comic."

"You'll soon wish you'd never heard of me!" barked Ed. "Did you give my comic to Rippa? Is that it?"

"No!" Charlie wailed.

"I told you, Charlie's was the second crime," I said. "It happened like this . . . Some time ago, you banned Charlie from your entire collection. Now, naturally, Charlie felt a bit put out by that. After all, the incident with the jelly was an accident. Right, Charlie?"

"Right," Charlie murmured into his hands.

"But, naturally, he was very curious to see *The Tomb of Death*. Your pride and joy. The most valuable collector's item he was probably ever going to set eyes on. But it was locked away in the safe.

"Now, Charlie here is a brighter guy than you give him credit for. He might not have known the combination to the safe, but he could work it out. He realized that you and your dad would have set it to something memorable. A significant date, a phone number . . . Right, Charlie?"

"Mom's birthday," mumbled Charlie.

Ed glanced at Charlie a couple of times in the rearview mirror. "How did you know that?"

"He didn't, at first," I said. "Over several days,

when nobody was around, he tried various combi-nations. Until he found the right one, last Sunday night. So he opened the safe and took out the comic. He only wanted to take a look at it, to read it and to see what all the fuss was about. He had every inten-tion of putting it right back. But almost as soon as he took it out of the safe, he realized he was in a world of doo-doo."

"So true," muttered Ed.

"Ed! Just listen to me," I said. The car wove ahead, overtaking a truck and changing lanes to pull away from a big SUV filled with fighting toddlers.

"As soon as Charlie looked through the comic, he realized it was fake. A dummy. A very good one, but a fake nonetheless."

"A *what*?" yelled Ed. "That's impossible! I know every square inch of that comic! Do you think I can't tell a fake when I see one?"

"We'll get to that," I said. "Keep your eyes on the road! What Charlie took from the safe was not the actual *Tomb of Death*. And when he realized that, he panicked. He had no idea what had happened to the real one. Would you think he'd taken it? Who *had* taken it? Had it always been a dummy? Were *you* hiding something?

"He didn't know what to do. Okay, with a bit more thought on his part, or by being honest from the beginning, things might have turned out better. But he was scared; he knew you'd be furious. For a start, there was nothing he could say without having to admit he'd gotten into the safe. And he figured he'd be in enough trouble for that, let alone whatever might happen because the comic was a fake.

"The point is, while he obsessed over what to do, the safe was reopened and the comic was discovered missing. Then you, Ed, told him to come and see me. Which, reluctantly, he did. And all this time, he was hiding away the fake comic.

"With Saxby Smart on the case, Charlie realized it was only a matter of time before he got found out. Which is true. He still had the fake comic in his backpack. So he went to the school office, distracted the secretary, and shredded the fake. Now, at least, when suspicions pointed toward him, there wasn't any physical evidence left."

"Wait a minute," said Charlie, finally uncovering his

face. "When you gave Ed those shreds of paper, you thought they might be the real comic, didn't you?"

"Ummm," I said, "yes, but anyway, moving on—"

"As if I'd do that," muttered Charlie.

"Moving on," I said quickly, "we now come to the *first* theft. The theft of the *real Tomb of Death*."

"By Rippa," said Ed.

"By Rippa." I nodded. "Izzy's research, and my own observations, had shown Rippa to be a shady dealer in more ways than one. He'd already tried to pass off a facsimile edition comic as the genuine article. He'd nearly succeeded too. So what more logical step is there for him than to go one better, and produce a really convincing fake, one that only an expert would spot? And why not aim high? Why not go for one of the most valuable comics there is? *The Tomb of Death* Issue 1.

"From various published sources, he could reproduce the comic's cover and inside pages. And there was a local dealer he knew, Ed Foster, who actually *had* a copy. If he played his cards right, he could go along and take a look at the real thing, to make sure his fake was as perfect as possible.

"The trouble was, he didn't have a good reputation

within the trade. He decided that once his fake was ready, he'd travel outside the Midwest, to one of the big American comics conventions where he wasn't known, and sell it there. In such a huge gathering, selling a super-valuable comic book might not attract much attention. So he worked away at his fake, and he managed to get you, Ed, to show him the real comic, for comparison. You said he had some magazines with him when he came to your house?"

"Yeah," said Ed.

"And tucked away inside one of them was his carefully made forgery. He only intended to get a close look at your comic. He knew you'd never allow him to borrow it or anything like that. But when the doorbell rang, and he was left alone in that room, he spotted the opportunity of a lifetime. Purely by luck, his forgery was on hand, and he made a snap decision. While you were gone, just for a few seconds, he swapped the real comic for his fake one. He gambled that when you came back in, you'd put the comic in the safe right away, without examining it closely. And that's exactly what you did. You assumed that was your comic back in its plastic cover. It wasn't. Rippa slipped the real

Tomb of Death in among his magazines, and he walked out with it, right under your nose."

"But he must have known I'd spot the forgery eventually," said Ed.

"Oh, eventually, yes," I said. "But he knew that normally, you never, ever took that comic out of the safe, let alone out of its protective cover. It might have stayed in there for months, or even years, before being discovered. I said to you when I examined the safe that only a stupid and desperate thief would try to snatch that comic, but I was wrong. Rippa took huge risks, but he wasn't an idiot.

"Think about it. If you, months or even years later, discovered the fake, and even if you linked that fake to Rippa, what actual evidence would you have? None. Even if you told the world, and ruined Rippa's reputation for good, he'd hardly mind, would he? He'd have sold the real comic and be living off a mountain of cash.

"He took a risk, and it seemed to pay off. The only problem was, he now had a genuine *Tomb of Death* and needed to get rid of it. He needed money to finance his trip to the convention, so he started selling off stock from his shop. He's been selling loads and buying little, to make sure he had enough money to take the trip as soon as possible. Today. And once he'd sold the comic . . . "

" . . . No evidence again," said Ed, grinding his teeth. "Unless I spent a fortune following the comic around the country, tracking its sale."

"Right," I said.

Ed signaled, and the car sped toward the exit off the highway. By the little clock that was Velcroed to the dashboard, the time was 3:22 p.m.

It was 3:27 p.m. when we raced into the parking lot opposite the airport's main entrance. Charlie and I hurried over to the terminal building while Ed hunted through the trash in the car's glove compartment for some change to pay for parking.

3:28 p.m. The glass doors slid open, and Charlie and I stepped into a swirling river of people, carts, and luggage. Tugging at Charlie's sleeve to get him to follow me, I headed straight for the enormous Departures screen, hanging above a nearby coffee stand.

3:29 p.m. "Let's see, let's see," I muttered. "Look for LAX. That's Los Angeles. No, wait, this is Arrivals. C'mon, c'mon, c'mon, LAX, LAX, LAX . . . I can't see it. Wait, the screen's changing . . . "

Charlie poked his head into view. "There's only one more flight to L.A. today; passengers have just been called to the gate—over there, Gate 22B."

I glanced back and forth between him and the screen. "That's genius. How'd you figure it out?"

"I asked that flight attendant over there."

"Ah, right," I said, nodding a thank you to a woman in a ghastly green uniform.

3:30 p.m.

We sped up a short staircase and across a wide area covered in shiny floor tiles and bolted-down seats. The departure lounge was directly ahead of us. Passengers were lining up at a row of scanners, ready to have their bags checked.

And there was Rippa! He was facing away from us, a carryon in one hand and a bag of chips in the other. He was almost at the front of the line.

"He hasn't seen us," said Charlie.

"But if he gets past those scanners, he's gone!" I said. "Airport security means we won't be able to follow him any farther!" We hurried toward him, worried about drawing attention to ourselves. If he spotted us now, all he'd have to do was leave the line and lose himself in the crowd. "Whatever you do," I whispered, "don't run. Don't make anyone in that line look around."

Suddenly, Ed overtook us, running like his butt was on fire, heading straight for Rippa. Charlie and I both made So-much-for-that!-faces.

But it was almost too late. Rippa was at the head of the line. In a few seconds, he'd be through the scanners. Even at full speed, Ed wouldn't reach him in time!

"How can we stop him?!" wailed Charlie.

For a split second, my mind went blank. But then I had a brilliant idea.

"Hey!" I shouted, at the top of my lungs. "Hey! Tarquin!"

The sound echoed off the flickering screens and the shiny floor. As one, every last person in sight turned to stare at me. Rippa, with a face like a mad bull, spun on his heels. Without a moment's thought, he flung his bag of chips right at me, his mouth twisted in a

wedge-shaped sneer. The chips bounced and skidded to a halt at my feet.

"So it's true," I said. "He really does throw things at people who call him that."

Rippa's pause gave Ed just enough time to reach him. Rippa almost made a run for it, but Ed took a firm hold of his arm and dragged him out of the line.

"Open it," said Ed, pointing to Rippa's carryon.

With his free hand, and a grunting sigh, Rippa unzipped the bag. Nestled inside, between some scrunched-up T-shirts and a pair of jeans, was a cardboard folder. Inside the folder was Issue 1 of *The Tomb of Death*.

"How did you know?" grunted Rippa.

"I didn't," said Ed. He pointed to me. "He did."

"And who are *you*?" sniffed Rippa, looking me up and down. "Sherlock freakin' Holmes?"

"No," I said with a smile. "My name is Saxby Smart."

On the way home, Charlie expected to get a giant, shouting lecture from his brother, but it seemed that Ed was a changed man. "I shouldn't have been so tough on you over the jelly, Charlie," he said, as the car chugged back to our town. "If I'd been less crabby, you might have come straight to me in the first place. Sorry."

"Does that mean I can read your collection?" said Charlie excitedly.

Ed said nothing for a while. "Dunno," he mumbled eventually. "I'll think about it."

Once I was home, I retreated to my shed. I made some notes on the case, and then I settled back in my Thinking Chair. There was a slight ripping sound from the arm. I sighed, and finally had to admit to myself that even a simple repair job like that was beyond me. I'd call my friend Muddy in the morning, I decided. Get a professional on it.

Case closed.

CASE FILE FIVE:

THE TREASURE OF
DEAD MAN'S LANE

SILAS MIDDLEMARCH

CHAPTER ONE

"Ohhh man," said Muddy. "Ohhhh man, oh man, oh man. Ohhhhhhh maaaan."

"Yeah, okay," I said grumpily. "Can you fix it?"

Muddy examined the rip in the arm of my Thinking Chair, prodding it with a grimy finger. "Ohhhh man. Yup, that's fixable. Should have called me in earlier, though, Saxby. You've let this develop into quite a nasty little tear."

"I can do without the lecture, thanks," I said. "I did try to fix it myself, you know."

"Yeah, I can tell," muttered Muddy, doing a bit more prodding. "What a mess. Tape, was it?"

"Just get on with it," I grumbled. "Stop enjoying yourself."

As I implied in the previous case, my great friend

George "Muddy" Whitehouse is a genius when it comes to practical and mechanical things. He goes around looking like he's been dragged through an assortment of puddles and ditches, but there's nobody at St. Egbert's School who's more skilled at fixing stuff. In less than ten minutes, there was a neatly glued patch on the arm of my Thinking Chair.

"Leave it for an hour or two before you sit in it," said Muddy, packing up his toolbox.

"Thanks," I said. "You know how important my Thinking Chair is. Do you want to stay for lunch?"

"Can't," said Muddy, with a gleam of excitement in his eyes. "I'm going over to The Horror House. I'm getting a tour this afternoon."

"You're joking," I gasped. "How? You've got to tell me!" Obviously, I couldn't see my own eyes right then, but I'm pretty certain they had a gleam of excitement in them too.

The Horror House was something of a local legend. If any building ever deserved a nickname, it was Number 13 Deadman's Lane. Imagine a spooky old house in a movie. Then imagine it much spookier. Then add a bit more spookiness for added effect, and you still wouldn't be anywhere near how utterly creepy this place looked.

It was a large, looming house, with huge bay windows on either side of a low-set front door, from which protruded an ornate, stone-columned porch. There were two upper floors, each with a series of tall, narrow windows that gave the impression of gapped teeth. The roof was sharply angled, topped with a ridge of crested tiles, and a couple of dormers poked out of it, looking like narrowed eyes above the grinning skulls of the windows below.

Nobody had lived at 13 Deadman's Lane for years. The place was boarded up, set back from the road behind a high fence of corrugated metal sheeting. People started calling it The Horror House because of its weird looks, and because it was an ideal reference point if you wanted to give someone directions to the mall ("Go straight past The Horror House and take a left at the light.").

"But how are you even getting in there?" I said. "It's all locked and barred."

"Not since Monday, it's not," said Muddy, grinning. "Jack's parents bought it."

"Jack Wilson, from class?" I said. "He sure kept that quiet."

"He didn't even know himself until Monday. His mom and dad didn't know if they'd get the money for it. They're going to fix it up and turn it into a hotel. Jack says his dad says they're up to their eyeballs in debt until they can renovate the whole place. The electricity hasn't been updated since 1955, and it's got a heating system dating back to 1937. A broken heating system, of course."

"Wow," I said. "I take it they're getting started right away?"

"The heating pipes got taken out on Tuesday," said Muddy. "Man, I'd love to get my hands on a bit of vintage material like that—it's too bad. They've been ripping out stuff every day. Which is lucky, really, because otherwise they wouldn't have found the secret scroll."

"Secret scroll?" I said, intrigued.

"Oh, Jack says his dad says it's not a real one. But it sounds like fun, all the same. It claims there's hidden treasure somewhere inside that building."

I steered Muddy out of the shed and into the house. "I want to hear more about this mysterious scroll," I said. "You've changed your mind, you're staying for lunch."

CHAPTER TWO

As Muddy and I sat at the kitchen table, picking at our astonishingly burnt grilled-cheese sandwiches, he told me about the parchment.

"Jack and his dad found it the other day," said Muddy, twisting the bread into shapes. "They were ripping out some old wooden wall panels in one of the upstairs rooms. The paneling had been put in when the house was built, about two hundred years ago, you can tell by looking at the wall behind it, apparently. But mold had recently gotten to it, and it was past saving. Anyway, they were stacking up all these big pieces of wood, and Jack suddenly noticed a sheet of paper wedged into a sort of slot at the back of one of the panels."

"A sort of slot?" I repeated.

"Jack's dad took a look at it," said Muddy. "There was a removable section in that panel, quite low down, behind a spot they'd removed a radiator from. A kind of hidden storage box, no bigger than a lunch box. They'd have never found it without removing all those panels."

"And this scroll is a treasure map?"

"Yeah. Well, it's not so much a map, more like a description of where the treasure is. Although apparently the description doesn't make much sense. Anyway, Jack says his dad says it's not as old as it looks. He thinks it was probably put there by the foster children."

"Foster children?" I said, chewing at a triangle of leftover crust.

"During World War Two the house was a shelter for kids whose parents were involved in the war effort. Tons of people have lived in that house over the years. It's only recently that it's been empty and run down."

"And those foster kids made the scroll?" I said.

"That's the theory. It's just the kind of thing a bunch of kids would do, isn't it? They come to live in a spooky old house, and they start making up games about hidden treasure and stuff. This piece of paper must've been left over from one of those games."

"And how did they find the hidden compartment?"

Muddy shrugged. "Just came across it one day, I guess. Then left their treasure map in there by mistake, maybe. Of course, it might not have been the foster kids at all. Could have been hippie radicals from the '60s or '70s or something. The house was still lived in until 1987. Anyway, Jack says his dad says it was most likely those children."

I thought hard for a minute or two. No, Jack's dad was definitely wrong. Perhaps he was distracted by the huge job he'd taken on, but there was an obvious flaw in his theory. From what Muddy had told me so far, I knew that the scroll had to be nearly a century old, at the very least. And I knew that those kids couldn't possibly have put it there: it was a question of historical events . . .

Have you spotted it?

Muddy had told me that the heating system dated back to 1937. He'd also told me that it had only been removed on Tuesday, the secret compartment being behind where a radiator had been fixed. Which meant that during the whole of World War Two, 1941–1945, the foster children couldn't have gotten to the compartment. In fact, *nobody* could have gotten to that compartment since 1937, so the scroll had to be at least that old, and possibly much older.

I decided then and there that learning dates for History class was useful after all!

"Come on," I said. "Let's take a look at that piece of paper. I think it could be perfectly genuine."

"Hang on," called Muddy, as I sped off, "I gotta finish my grilled cheese!"

CHAPTER THREE

"Now *that* is spooky," I whispered.

"It's like it's looking back at you," Muddy replied.

The Horror House stood like a huge, crouching goblin. It was set back from the road, and surrounded by a gnarling, overgrown yard. Behind it, we could see the tops of the trees in the wooded area that led down to the local river. (Those woods were equally gloomy, and had an equally sinister nickname: The Hangman's Lair. I once solved a very puzzling mystery there. I might write up my notes on that case one day.)

Number 13 stood well away from the other houses on Deadman's Lane, as if it was being snooty and didn't want to talk to its neighbors. The tall sheets of corrugated metal that had fenced in the house for as long as I could remember had all been torn down. They were

stacked in a huge heap amid the tangle of thistles and thorns that stuck to us as Muddy and I walked up the cracked driveway to the front door.

Jack Wilson greeted us like an excited puppy. The human equivalent of an excited puppy, I mean. He didn't lick our faces. Or have a tail to wag. Or bark. But you get the idea. Jack's a round, bouncy boy, with a face that always looks like he's just gotten some really good news. He ushered us into a large, shadowy front hall.

"Wowww," gasped Muddy, taking it all in.

"So this is The Horror House," I said, gazing up at the high ceiling.

"It's re*volt*ing," breathed Muddy, eyeing the cracked plaster and the peeling paint and the moldy shreds of wallpaper clinging in miserable patches above the high wainscoting.

"Yeah, it's not too great at the moment," agreed Jack. "Still, if it was beautifully decorated, we'd have been calling it The Lovely House all these years, wouldn't we? Look out for that floorboard, Saxby, it's rotten. Mom put her foot straight through it yesterday. I laughed till I cried."

Sounds of heavy-duty machinery were echoing from

somewhere upstairs. We picked our way carefully up the wide, curved staircase and waited on the landing until the loud sawing noises stopped and the cloud of dust that was drifting out of one of the bedrooms subsided.

Jack's dad emerged from the dusty haze, wielding a huge circular saw. The saw's battered power cord hung from his other hand like a lasso. From the heels of his boots to the bald patch on his head, he was caked in a mixture of sawdust, white plaster dust, and more sawdust.

"Hello," he said, grinning. "Watch where you step."

"The rotten floorboards?" asked Muddy.

"No, our rotten cat. Dirty little scamp," said Jack's dad. "He sees a pile of sawdust and thinks it's a litter box. S'cuse me, I've got to knock out some old plaster before Jack's mom gets back from the hardware store. Then I've got the man from the Building Department coming. Then I've got to find the broom I left around here somewhere."

"Yeah, the floor could use a good sweep," said Jack.

"No, I was going to whack the cat with it," muttered Jack's dad. "Dirty little scamp, he repeated."

We left Jack's dad to work his way through his To-

Do list. The sound of a sledgehammer breaking stuff followed us along the hallway. As Jack showed us into a large, dusty room overlooking the street, Muddy told him about our conversation.

"You really think that scroll is as old as the house?" said Jack. Our shoes crunched against the grit that littered the bare floor.

"We know it must predate 1937," I said. "And if that storage compartment was as well hidden and as precisely sized as Muddy says, then it's quite possible that it was built into the wood paneling specifically to hide that one piece of paper."

"That's a little extreme, isn't it?" said Muddy. "To build a compartment into a wall just for that? If what's written on the paper is that secret, why write it down at all? Why not just memorize it?"

"Exactly," said Jack. "It's a spooky-sounding bunch of nonsense that someone made up and hid years and years ago, giggling away, knowing that someone else would come along and get all excited about it. It really is just gobbledegook. I think you're wrong, Saxby, I think it's a long-lost practical joke."

"This is the room you found it in?" I said. It was a

large but unremarkable room, with two tall windows—two of those "teeth" in the front face of the building—and an irregularly shaped wood stove built into one corner.

"I've got it over here," said Jack. From the deep windowsill he grabbed a box file, the kind of solid cardboard bin for holding papers that you see in offices. He flipped it open and handed it to me.

Inside it was a sheet of thick paper, about twelve inches high and six inches wide. Its left-hand edge was slightly jagged, the others neatly cut. It was yellowed with age, with brownish spots and blotches here and there across its surface, but it was surprisingly smooth and substantial to the touch. Obviously very expensive paper (the exact opposite of the kind encountered in the case of *The Tomb of Death!*).

On the paper, in angular but flowing handwriting, were lines written in black ink, all neatly aligned on the page. The words had clearly been written with one of those old-fashioned dip-in-the-ink pens: you could see where the ink kept thinning out every few words, then suddenly became thicker again when the pen was dipped. In all, it said:

Now, three by itself of eighth, solar revolutions twenty from Bonaparte's fall, and nine, I hereby veil my dark and mighty treasure.

Through its right eye, it sees a bullet-line down half a corner.

Through its left eye, the canvas.

Bisect and again, and lo! the needle's mark, Rome's war-god steps to the circle's edge.

Eastward the sky, westward the earth, northward we go and beneath.

Mirror the prize and see the trees, fall from the glass and feel the soil.

Down, and down, and where the saucer goes, go I.

SM

"Well," said Jack, reading the paper again over my shoulder, "I've come across some pretty strange clues for scavenger hunts, but this takes the cake! It's nonsense. It's a joke, it has to be."

"It's not nonsense," I said, peering closely at the scroll in the gray light from the window. "It's simply a complicated puzzle. It leads to this 'dark and mighty treasure,' I'm sure of it. It's far too elaborate to be nothing more than a practical joke."

"Okay, then, make some sense out of just one line," said Jack. "Show me exactly what one line means, and I'll believe you."

I read through the words again. They certainly seemed to defy logic! But, assuming that I was right and they *did* actually mean something, it was possible to make a guess about what the first line might mean. After all, if you were writing an important document, what would you be most likely to put at the top?

"I can tell you the exact date this was written," I said.

"Oh yeah?" said Jack.

"Oh yeah," I said. "I just need to check a historical fact."

I flipped open my phone and called The Fountain of All Knowledge (or Izzy, as she prefers to be called). "Quick fact check," I said. "Think you could look up the date on which Napoleon Bonaparte was finally defeated?"

"Who?" muttered Muddy.

"French guy. Late eighteenth century, early nineteenth," I said. "I think. If I'm remembering what I read in *The Boy's Big Book of Facts* correctly."

There was a click on the line as Izzy returned. "Battle of Waterloo," she said. "1815. Is something interesting going on?"

"Something very interesting indeed. I'll get back to you. I may need a lot of background info for this one."

I pocketed my phone, turned to Jack, and pointed

out the first line on the treasure "map," up to the part that said "my dark and mighty treasure."

"There's the date," I said. My math is generally about as strong as a soggy tissue, but with a bit of lateral thinking and a bit of simple math, I could see that the first part of the sentence was a date and a month. And then, using a bit more math and a bit of general scientific knowledge, I could see that the second part of the sentence gave a year.

Can you work it out?

"This was written in August 1844," I said.

Now, three by itself of eighth, solar revolutions twenty from Bonaparte's fall, and nine . . .

"Three by itself of eighth," I said. "Our whoever-it-was is putting the date at the top of his work. 'Three by itself' could simply be the number three, on its own? But not if this is meant to be a puzzle! That would be far too easy. No, I think it's three times itself, three times three. Nine. Of course, I can't be sure of that, but I bet that's probably it. And 'of eighth'? Of the eighth month? August."

"Hmm, s'pose so," said Jack doubtfully.

"Next, the year. 'Solar revolutions'? Well, one revolution of the sun means one year, right? We did that in Science ages ago, right? So, twenty years from 'Bonaparte's fall,' and then another nine. Napoleon was defeated in 1815, add twenty-nine to that, and you get 1844."

"Why not take away twenty-nine?" said Muddy.

"Because you'd be dating your document *before* 'Bonaparte's fall,'" said Jack, "and that wouldn't make sense, because you wouldn't know about it."

"Right," I said. "Do you believe me now? These words do mean something. I think they lead to something important!"

"You may be right after all," whispered Jack.

"Maybe there's a chest full of gold!" said Muddy. "A pirate's hoard or something."

"I think 1844's a little late for pirates," I said. "But you never know. . . . "

We stared at each other with our eyes bugging out, our jaws dropping, and our feet skipping around as though we were a bunch of overexcited horses. There was a secret treasure in The Horror House, a treasure that had been hidden away for many years, and *we were going to find it!*

What can I deduce about that scroll—or rather, the person who wrote it? He (or she)...

1. ...was the neat and tidy type. Those lines were written so straight and even, and carefully centered on the page. But! How significant is that tear on the left side? Was the paper ripped out of something? Or was something removed from it?

2. ...was smart, to come up with such obviously complex riddles.

3. ...probably had a reason to be afraid. Otherwise, why go to such trouble to conceal the treasure? But afraid of what? Of whom? And why? If the treasure is stolen gold or something like that, then the answers are obvious. But is that the whole story?

4. ...had the initials SM!

PROBLEM: Muddy made a good point—if the treasure was such a secret, why make a path to it at all? Why not simply commit the location of the treasure to memory?

ANSWER: He/she must have intended to pass on the treasure.

PROBLEM: Why pass it on using such strange methods?

PROBLEM: The way the "map" is written must have been designed to be understood by whomever it was intended for, but to seem like obscure gobbledegook to whomever it wasn't meant for. That could be important. Must think about this some more.

CHAPTER FOUR

The next day was Saturday. Muddy and I arrived back at the house at 9:00 a.m., ready for a solid day's treasure hunt. Muddy brought along a backpack full of assorted gadgets he'd designed. I wasn't sure how useful the Whitehouse Silent Alarm Mark II or the Whitehouse Personal Reversing Mirror might turn out to be, but I thought having a few tools on hand was a good idea nonetheless.

Izzy turned up at a quarter past nine. When I called her back the night before and gave her the full story, I also sent her a copy of the scroll. Jack's parents had been given a pile of old documents when they'd bought the house: legal stuff, plans showing where the drains were, a certificate from when the plumbing was installed, that kind of stuff. None of it helped us decipher the scroll, and none of it recorded anything earlier than 1900. So I was counting on Izzy to come up with a find!

Us boys were all in ratty jeans and sweatshirts, because we were expecting to get as dusty as Jack's dad, but Izzy showed up in her usual get-up, all glistening curls and snazzy colors. "You'll ruin those pants," I said, raising an eyebrow.

"I'm not staying," said Izzy. "I only came over to get a closer look at The Horror House. I've got tons of leads for information, but I need to go to the library and search the local records. Wow, this place is a dump."

"A dump with hidden treasure," corrected Muddy.

"A dump that *might* have hidden treasure," corrected Jack.

We trudged across the hallway, our boots kicking up delicate clouds of plaster dust. Various *thumps* and *clanks* and *ka-chuggs* echoed from other parts of the house: Jack's mom was busy shoveling sand into the rented cement mixer in the backyard, and Jack's dad was busy chasing the cat. As we all sat at the bottom of the staircase, I took out the photocopy of the scroll I'd made and read through it for the thirty-seventh time.

"What've you got so far?" I said to Izzy.

Izzy grabbed a printout from inside the plastic folder she was carrying. "This house was built in 1837, by a man named Silas Middlewich."

"SM!" said Muddy.

"Originally, it was a workhouse, a kind of half prison where poor people ended up when they had nowhere else to go. They were terrible places. This street was originally called Mill Lane, but once the workhouse was here, everyone started calling it Deadman's Lane, because it was said that nobody left here alive."

"And over time, Dead Man's Lane became Deadman's Lane," I said.

Izzy nodded. "I want to do a lot more research on this Silas Middlewich, but it looks like he was an A-grade Mr. Nasty. He packed more and more people into this place and forced them to work for him until he was the richest man in the district. He died in 1845; it's said he was murdered by one of his workers, a woman named Martha Humble. Apparently he'd swindled her husband."

"Nice guy," I muttered.

"Still, someone like that is exactly the type of person who might've hidden his ill-gotten gains in a secret stash," said Muddy excitedly.

I wasn't so sure. I thought back on my notes, about deductions that could be made from the scroll. Something didn't add up.

"You could be right," said Izzy. "But there's a vital point you're all missing. Saxby's theory about that secret compartment must be wrong."

"I beg your pardon?" I said, looking up suddenly.

"The wall paneling was built at the same time as the house. Which we now know was 1837. But you've worked out that the scroll is dated 1844. So the compartment was there for seven years, empty. Doesn't make sense."

"Hmm," I said, getting a sinking feeling. "I don't get it. That compartment was perfectly sized for the scroll in both height and width."

"Perhaps the compartment was originally used to hide the treasure, but then it got moved?" Muddy guessed.

"No," I said. "The compartment was only an inch or two deep. Not big enough."

"Plus," said Izzy, in a way that sounded reluctant, "why would someone like Middlewich leave a treasure trail for someone to follow? If he was as nasty as his reputation suggests, he wouldn't want anyone getting their hands on his cash, would he?"

"Ugh! Well, so much for a great start," said Jack. "You really got up my hopes there, Saxby."

I held up my hand for silence. I was trying to think. What Izzy had just said was absolutely right. There was another layer of mystery here: there was a strange difference between what I had worked out about the scroll and what Izzy had found out about this Silas Middlewich. We'd found a weird gap in history!

One thing was certain. It was even more vital now that we decipher the scroll. There were more secrets here than buried treasure alone.

I jumped to my feet. "Muddy, Jack, we're getting to work on the scroll, right now. Izzy, to the library. Find out all you can, and get back to us as soon as possible."

CHAPTER FIVE

"Okay, the first line is the date; let's work on the second," I said.

Through its right eye, it sees a bullet–line down half a corner . . .

"What's 'it'?" said Muddy.

"What's 'half a corner'?" said Jack.

"If I'm understanding Silas Middlewich's way of working correctly," I said, "'half a corner' probably means half a right angle. Forty-five degrees. Basic math again."

"What's 'it'?" said Muddy.

"So, by 'a bullet-line,' do you think he just means a

straight line?" said Jack. "The line that a bullet would take?"

"I think that's highly likely," I said.

"Hellooooo?" wailed Muddy. "What's 'it'? And where's 'its right eye'?"

"I have absolutely no idea," said Jack.

"Neither do I." I shrugged. But suddenly, the answer hit me harder than a brick wrapped in concrete. My mind flashed back to the previous day, when Muddy and I had arrived at Deadman's Lane. Immediately, I knew exactly where this eye was, and what it belonged to.

Have you spotted it?

I dashed outside, the others following. At the edge of the pavement, I turned and pointed up at the windows.

"It's the house itself!" I said. "You know how it seems to have a face? That window up there, poking out of the roof. The house's right eye!"

"Bingo!" cried Jack. "But . . . that's its left eye."

"No, the scroll says 'it sees a bullet-line.' It does the seeing. From the house's point of view, that's its right eye."

We dashed back inside, and up to the room with the "right eye" for a window. It was a small, cobweb-covered room, with a sharply angled ceiling and two floorboards missing in one corner.

"Now, a straight line from the window, looking down at a forty-five degree angle," I said.

Muddy almost yelped with excitement. From his backpack he produced an ordinary protractor and the viewfinder mechanism from an old camera, onto which he'd stenciled the words FlixiScope Model B.

"Will this help?" he asked.

"Not 100 percent accurate, but it'll do," I said.

Muddy held the protractor, Jack judged the angle, and, squinting with one eye, I looked through the viewfinder. Directly in its crosshairs was an empty paper bag marked DIY Warehouse Readymix Concrete, which must have been blown around the side of the house and gotten caught in the front yard.

"We're in luck," I said. "That bag marks the exact spot."

We dashed back outside. By now I was getting out of breath, and telling myself I really ought to get more exercise.

We picked our way across the tangled, thorny jungle of a front yard until we found the empty bag. Muddy stood right at its center, exactly where the viewfinder had pointed.

Through its left eye, the canvas.

"Okay, Muddy, now look up at the house's left-eye window," I said. "What do you see?"

"Nothing," said Muddy.

"What can 'the canvas' be?" asked Jack. "A painting?"

"Possibly," I said. "But I think it's probably something else. I doubt the trail would rely on having a specific object put in a specific place."

"Why?" said Muddy.

"Because something like that could change so easily," I said. "You'd only have to move the painting and the whole puzzle would fall apart. Silas Middlewich must be referring to something that probably wouldn't change over time. What can you see, Muddy?"

"Nothing. Just the window."

"And through it?"

"Just the facing wall."

"Well, that's it then!" I cried. "A big blank wall! You could call that a canvas, right?"

We dashed back inside again. Now I was really getting out of breath and wishing I'd made more of an effort during PE.

The far wall in the "left eye" room was tall and rectangular. The pale yellow paint that covered it was darkened around the edges with age, and there was a slightly lighter, sharply defined patch to one side, where a heavy piece of furniture must have stood for many years.

Bisect and again, and lo !
the needle's mark, Rome's war —
god steps to the circle's edge.

"Now what's that supposed to mean?" said Jack.

"Bisect," I muttered. "More math. That's geometry."

"Yeah, bisecting means dividing in two, doesn't it?" said Muddy.

"So we're looking for an area of the wall," said Jack.

"An exact point, rather than an area," I said. "It says 'the needle's mark.' The mark a needle would leave is a point."

"Right," said Jack. "'Bisect and again,' that must mean we divide it twice. And if we want to find a point, that means we have to draw the lines in opposite directions, so that they cross. But how are we supposed to do the dividing? Floor to ceiling? Corner to corner?"

"Doesn't matter," I said. "It must mean the exact center. Whichever way you halve the wall, top to bottom or corner to corner, you'll get the same thing. The center."

Hurriedly, Muddy retrieved a marker and a ball of string from his bag. Standing on a packing crate, I held one end of the string at the wall's top left corner, Jack held the other end at the bottom right, and Muddy traced the line. Once the second line was drawn, bottom left to top right, we had our mark!

We stepped back. None of us said anything, but there was a tangible sense of nervous anticipation in the room, an eager thrill of discovery.

Rome's war-god steps to the circle's edge.

"Logically, we now have to go somewhere else, away from the center point we just marked," I said. "And the next line on the scroll implies that we go to the edge of a circle. Or at least, I think that's what it implies."

"With the center point as the center of the circle?" said Jack.

"But how big a circle?" said Muddy.

We stood there for a moment, pondering. The late-morning sun threw geometric shapes of light across the wall.

"I wonder if this part about 'Rome's war-god' is a measurement . . . " I said, more to myself than the others. "A measurement of the size of the circle, maybe?"

"Well, the Roman god of war was Mars," said Jack. "We know that from last year, learning about Ancient Rome. But we need a number—not a name."

"The Romans used letters for numbers!" Muddy suddenly cried. "Is that it?"

"No," said Jack. "The only letter they used in 'Mars' was M, and that equaled one thousand. A thousand of anything would be too big a measurement to fit on the wall."

"How about the planet Mars?" I said. "Our friend Silas seems to like these little cross-references, doesn't he? Mars is the fourth planet. Wait a sec, is it? Um . . . Mercury, Venus, Earth . . . yes, Mars is the fourth, definitely. There's a possible number."

"Yeah, but four what?" said Jack. "What's the unit of measure? Oh man, look at us—doing math in our spare time! Mrs. Penzler would be delighted!"

"Four . . . 'steps,' presumably," I said, frowning. "'Rome's war-god steps to the circle's edge.'"

"But how big a step?" said Jack. "It all depends on how long your legs are!"

"And how do we walk across the wall to measure them?" said Muddy.

"It can't literally mean steps," I said. "Remember, this is a riddle. The word *step* must somehow translate into our missing unit of measure. Silas must've wanted to indicate something standard, something that would be meaningful to whoever was meant to follow the trail, something that in 1844 would be—"

I stopped mid-sentence. My eyes darted to Muddy's backpack.

"Muddy, have you got a ruler?"

Muddy quickly rummaged in the bag. He pulled out a round, chunky object and handed it over.

"Muddy," said Jack, "that's just a tape measurer with a label saying Whitehouse Measure-Tek 2000!"

"Shut up!" said Muddy. "It does the job!"

I pulled out a length of the metal measuring tape and twisted it over to read the markings printed on its yellow surface.

"Of course, feet and inches!" I cried. "Plain old feet and inches—how could I have missed it? The measurement is four feet! That's the radius!"

"Huh?" said Jack.

"I told you, 'steps' must indicate a unit of measure," I said. "What do you step with? Feet. Four feet to the circle's edge. Stupid pun, but it works."

With the tape measure locked at the right length, and keeping one end of the tape positioned over the center of the wall, we drew a huge circle.

"Hey, we're really getting somewhere," said Muddy with a grin.

"I guess the next line tells us where on the circle to look," I said. "What direction to take from the center."

Eastward the sky, westward the earth, northward we go and beneath.

"Oh yeah?" said Jack. "How? The sky isn't east, no matter where you are."

I was on a roll! I spotted it at once. Standing back, looking at the circle we'd drawn on the wall, I was reminded of a slightly off-center compass. And suddenly, the answer was obvious.

Can you see it?

"Look at the wall," I said. "We want a direction. 'Eastward the sky,' it says. Twist the points of the compass so that, as drawn on this particular wall, east is up. That puts west at the bottom."

"Toward the earth," said Muddy. "'Westward the earth.'"

Jack groaned and slapped his face.

"Northward, then, points left," I said. "Follow that to the edge of the circle, and we arrive here." I tapped the "northerly" edge of the circle.

"So what does 'and beneath' mean?" Jack asked. "Where do we go now?"

"Into the wall," I said simply. "If north is to the left, then beneath is thataway."

"Awesome!" cried Muddy. "Demolition!"

He rooted around his backpack and pulled out what looked like a metal cylinder fixed into a wire frame. "I only just developed this. It doesn't even have a name yet. The digger is pushed forward by this spring, which came from an old couch, and when you switch it on, it starts—"

"Is this some kind of drill?" I said.

"Yup," said Muddy proudly. "The lever here adjusts the—"

"Isn't this just the tiniest bit dangerous?" I said.

"Only if you're stupid with it," said Muddy. "It was designed to cut holes in grass, for playing golf. But it should work okay on plaster. The only problem is, at the moment the battery lasts for just six and a half seconds. Needs some work."

Jack and I stepped back a little. Then we stepped back a little more. Muddy held the wire frame against the correct spot on the wall. Jack and I stepped back a little more.

Muddy switched his invention on, and the metal cylinder started to rotate inside the frame. Six and a half seconds later, the machine whined to a halt, and a shower of old plaster was tumbling out of a neatly cut hole halfway up the wall.

"You know, Muddy," I muttered, "you really are a genius."

I blew a layer of dust out of the hole and peered in. Visible behind the plaster were a couple of thin wooden struts, and tucked behind those, almost out of sight, was something metallic. I scratched at it with my finger, gradually pulling it free, and at last it dropped into the palm of my hand. It was a key, about the same length as my thumb. I held it up for the others to see.

"I don't believe it," gasped Jack. "We've been absolutely right."

"You know what this means, don't you?" giggled Muddy. "That must be the key to the treasure chest! There really is treasure at the end of all this!"

I had to admit, things were looking good. I stared wide-eyed at the key, amazed that this little object had been hidden away from the world for so long. For decade after decade, through wars and winters and world events. I felt as if it had been handed to me across the centuries, from Silas Middlewich in 1844 to me, here, now, today.

"Come on, guys," I said quietly. "Two more lines to go. We've got work to do."

CHAPTER SIX

"What's the next one?" said Jack.

> *Mirror the prize and see the trees, fall from the glass and feel the soil.*

"Well, 'the prize' must mean the key," I said.

"Are we supposed to look at it in a mirror?" said Muddy. "And even if we did, how would we see a tree?"

I turned the key over and over in my fingers, examining it closely. It was a perfectly ordinary key, without markings or oddities of any kind. It wasn't particularly light or heavy, and it didn't seem to be made of anything unusual.

"It's obviously got something to do with mirroring or symmetry, but what?" I mumbled.

"Math again," sighed Jack.

"Maybe it's a reflection instead of a mirror," said Muddy. "The next part of the line mentions glass, and that reflects."

I snapped my fingers. Which I only did because I couldn't get a huge exclamation point to ping into view above my head. "We're thinking too small. Most of what we've done so far has involved the house itself, and moving around in it. We're now standing as far as you can go on this side of the house. If we mirror the exact spot we found the key in on the other side of the house, what do we get?"

As one, we charged out of the room and across the landing at the top of the stairs. Keeping in mind a careful three-dimensional picture of the key's hiding place, we hurried across the house, judged the correct position as closely as we could, and found ourselves at the end of a corridor, standing in front of a window.

"A side window," said Jack. "'Mirror the prize and see the trees'!"

"But you can't see any trees from here," said Muddy,

peering out and making a face. "All you can see is the cloverleaf and the mall."

"I thought I heard you guys stomping around." At that moment, Izzy appeared in the hallway, clutching a pile of papers to her chest.

"Perfect timing!" I cried. "Did you find any photos?"

"Of . . . ?"

"Of the house in the 1840s?" I said. "I need to confirm a theory."

"Actually, yes," said Izzy. "I was able to find loads of stuff, along with a very talkative old lady behind the desk, who happened to be something of a local historian. Here, there are some pictures in with all this." She handed me the papers, and I started flipping through them eagerly.

"Wow, Izzy—incredible," I said, still zipping through one sheet after another. "This mystery's got more questions than two trivia books and a game show put together! Give us the highlights."

"Okay," Izzy began. "Tonight's headlines. Silas Middlewich came from a very poor family. Which, the way I see it, makes his running a workhouse here all the more shameful, exploiting poor people like that. He got his money—the money to build this place—by getting involved in buying and selling local plots of land. These deals were highly illegal, it seems. Dozens of wealthy townspeople were involved, including the mayor, a Mr. Carmichael, and a factory owner named Isaac Kenton, but nothing was ever proven. It's thought that Middlewich covered up the whole thing. It's also thought that Middlewich murdered Isaac Kenton's wife. She vanished without a trace in 1844, the same year this document was written. Again, nothing was ever proven."

"And Middlewich himself was murdered?" said Jack.

"Yes, in 1845," said Izzy, "by this Martha Humble I mentioned before. Nothing more is known about her, only that she accused him of swindling her husband, whoever he was. Anyway, Middlewich was so hated around town that the local teacher, a man named Josiah Flagg, started a kind of anti-Middlewich committee. The town constable, Mr. Trottman, even had this house raided twice, looking for evidence against Middlewich. But Middlewich was obviously too good at covering his tracks. I'm telling you, Jack, your parents own a house built by a total crook."

"I'm not so sure," I muttered to myself. I stopped sorting through Izzy's papers and looked up at the three of them. "I know who this treasure hunt was meant for. I know who Silas Middlewich wanted to leave his treasure to."

"Who?" said Muddy.

"Think about how the scroll's written, about how we've gone about deciphering it. From what Izzy's told us, there was a certain person who would've had an easier time following this than most people. In 1844, anyway."

Have you figured out who it was?

"The teacher, Josiah Flagg," I said. "Every single clue we've followed has involved exactly the kind of math, science, and history that we learn about today. Most people in 1844 had no real education at all. Most people would've gotten hopelessly stuck somewhere along the trail."

"No way," said Izzy. "He hated Middlewich. Let's face it: everyone hated Middlewich. That can't be right."

"Silas Middlewich left this trail for someone to follow," I said.

"Even the great Saxby Smart can make one too many assumptions, you know," she said, eyeing me with a sly smile.

"You just wait," I said, eyeing her right back. I turned to the window, brandishing one of the pieces of paper Izzy had brought. "Voilà!" I declared. "The trees!"

I showed them what Izzy had photocopied at the library. It was an engraving, dated 1860, showing the house from a short distance away. Along with the woods behind the building, there were thickly wooded areas on both sides, too.

"If you'd have looked out this window in 1844, all you would've seen would have been trees, trees, and more trees. You'd probably still have seen trees in 1944."

"Right," said Jack. "So, now . . ."

. . . fall from the glass and feel the soil.

We slid the window open, peered out, and looked straight down. A "fall from the glass" would have landed us in the yard. Well, it might've done so in 1844. But not anymore.

"Oh man," said Muddy quietly.

We were looking at the large clear roof of a greenhouse, added to the side of the house by a more recent owner. Two minutes later, we were looking at that same roof from below. Then we looked down at the rock-hard, concrete floor beneath our sneakers.

Down, and down, and where the saucer goes, go I.

"It says 'down and down,'" wailed Muddy. "We can't go down through this. Not without some seriously heavy equipment."

"I don't *believe* it!" Jack growled furiously. He stomped the floor as hard as he could. It was so solid, the blow barely made a sound.

"Isn't there a basement?" I asked.

"Yeah, but it's toward the back of the house," said Jack.

Suddenly, Izzy twitched as if she'd just been poked with a stick. "Wait! Wait!" She quickly rifled through the papers she was carrying, tossing pages aside as she went. "In with all those documents your parents got with the house, Jack! Plans of the sewers!"

"I am *not* going down a sewer!" cried Jack.

"Of course!" I said. "That plan would detail everything under the house."

Izzy found the document she was looking for and excitedly tapped a finger against it. "Look! Look!"

"The basement goes all the way across here," I said, tracing the line that marked its edges. "It extends out past the side of the house, including this spot we're standing on right now. We *can* go down from here."

Without a moment's hesitation, we raced for the cellar, clattering down a flight of wooden steps into a long, low room lit only by a single bare light bulb hanging above us. *Then* we hesitated.

"Ugh, it stinks," said Izzy.

"It's very damp," said Jack. "Dad says it'll be the biggest job in the house, getting it right. It's going to be used as a boiler room and laundry."

"We've got to go over to that far corner," I said. "That's the section under the greenhouse."

The basement was mostly empty. A few decaying wooden crates were stacked up to one side, leaning against the wall's moist bricks as though they were too exhausted to stand on their own. Our shoes made dull scraping sounds against the shiny gray flagstone floor. The single light bulb beamed clawlike shadows around us as we moved.

Once we were in the right spot, we took a good look around.

. . . and where the saucer goes, go I.

"But there's nothing here," Jack said quietly. His voice sounded thick and heavy, as if the dampness of the walls soaked it up as he spoke. "Where the heck would you put a saucer?"

"I assume he meant, like, a china tea-set saucer," said Muddy. "Not a flying saucer."

"I don't think they had aliens in 1844," said Izzy, making a face at the patch of mossy stuff growing on the bricks beside her.

I was also feeling puzzled, to say the least. But that last line *had* to be about something down here. I took another close look at everything around me:

1. The ceiling: Made up of gray panels that had been nailed in place; obviously not the original ceiling, but a more modern covering of some kind, bashed and gouged in several places.

2. The floor: Plain, gray flagstones; in some places, almost slippery with dampness; some of them worn down into a dipping, uneven surface, one stone worn so deeply you could put your foot in it; with scattered dirt and rusty discarded nails.

3. The walls: The same plain bricks used on the walls in the rest of the house; dark and damp, several of them in a crumbly, flaky state, forming a kind of dotted line at knee height; the mortar joints between them dotted with black.

"Of course," I whispered. "I see it now. It's one of Silas's sideways-thinking clues. All you've got to do is ask yourself, 'What does a saucer go under?'"

Do you see it too?

I crouched down and pointed to that deeply eroded stone in the floor. "'Where the saucer goes, go I.' A saucer goes under a cup. That flagstone is worn into . . ."

"Something pretty close to a cup shape!" said Izzy.

"Muddy," I said, looking up at him. "Got something to lift it up?"

Muddy produced a large screwdriver from his bag and crouched down too, pushing the flat end of it as deep into the crack at the edge of the flagstone as he could. With a few heaves, the stone was lifted. It flipped over with a loud *k-klak*. Beneath it, surrounded by earth, was what could only be the lid of a small wooden chest.

"That's it!" cried Jack.

"The treasure!" cried Muddy.

I, being me, didn't want to start sinking my hands into the dirt. Yuck! But Muddy, being Muddy, dived right in, digging the box free. At last, he hauled it up out of the hole he'd dug and set it down on the stone floor.

It wasn't very large, but it was very degraded. Over the years, the wide metal straps that reinforced its edges had become pitted and discolored. The wood it was made from had been half-eaten away by the earth and whatever lived down there.

I took the key we'd found out of my pocket and handed it to Jack. "It'd probably split open with a good kick," I said, "but I think this is more appropriate."

With a grin, Jack kneeled down and twisted aside the small metal plate that covered the lock. The rest of us hardly dared to breathe, our hearts racing. The key turned, and with a crunching sound, the lock sprang open.

Jack lifted the lid. Inside, tightly wrapped in cloth for preservation, was a leather-bound notebook. We

stood around him as he flipped through it. Every page was filled with handwriting, lists, and numbers. Toward the back of it was a torn edge, where a page had been ripped out. Inside the front cover, in the same familiar lettering as the scroll, were the words:

Journal of
Mr. Silas Middlewich,
begun 4 June 1837,
ended 7 August 1844.

"That's it?" said Jack. "That's the treasure of Dead Man's Lane?"

"It certainly is," I said, smiling wide. "It certainly is."

CHAPTER SEVEN

Izzy, Muddy, Jack, Jack's parents, and I assembled in the rubble-strewn spot that was going to be the house's main dining area, once the renovation was completed. It had been a week since we'd unearthed Silas Middlewich's journal, and I now had the means to put right a great injustice.

The others sat on upturned packing crates. I stood in front of them, holding the journal.

"We thought we'd find gold and jewels," I began. "Or something similar. You're all still asking yourselves: so, what actually happened to Silas Middlewich's ill-gotten gains? Where *did* he hide all that cash he'd squeezed out of those he'd swindled? The answer is: he never had any in the first place."

"What?" said Izzy. "That completely contradicts everything that's known about him."

"Exactly," I said. "Everything that's known about him is wrong. This journal proves it, and in light of what it says, I noticed some significant holes in those old documents and newspaper articles Izzy found—a lot more speculation that actual facts—and those sources are what that history-buff librarian Izzy talked to would've been going by. Silas Middlewich had a reputation as a crook and a cruel workhouse owner, but in reality he was the exact opposite. He was a champion of the poor. This house, the workhouse he built, was used to shelter destitute people. He put every penny he had into keeping them safe and properly fed."

"But how, then, could he get such a terrible reputation?" said Jack.

"Izzy discovered," I said, "that he got the money to build this place from some shady land deals with local bigwigs. That much is true. I can't say I follow all the legal ins and outs of it, but basically, the bigwigs were illegally buying and selling each other's land. According to some correspondence Middlewich copied into the journal, they *knew* what they were doing was against the law, but they *thought* Middlewich was on their side. He wasn't. It was brilliant, really. He had them paying him all kinds of rents and allowances, and they couldn't do a thing about it because every last deal they'd signed would've landed them in jail."

"So, these landowners started calling him a crook?" said Jack.

"Exactly," I said. "They couldn't go to the police, so they used their influence to try and ruin Silas Middlewich some other way."

"Hang on," said Izzy. "Surely what Middlewich did was wrong too? I mean, he *did* swindle those landowners, even if he did it with the best intentions."

"Absolutely right," I explained. "But he realized that these wealthy landowners had a lot more to lose than he did, if it all went public. He wasn't interested in his reputation. He didn't care who called him a crook. He'd been born into a poor family, and he saw it as his mission in life to help others in the same position. He was a kind of Victorian Robin Hood!"

"So where does the hidden treasure come in?" said Jack's dad, a scattering of plaster dust falling lightly from his hair.

"Ah!" I said, holding up the journal. "It wasn't long before the landowners were plotting among themselves how to have Middlewich run out of town. Of course, they wouldn't do their own dirty work, so they persuaded the local schoolteacher to organize efforts against Middlewich."

"Josiah Flagg," said Muddy.

"Right," I said. "But Middlewich stayed put. Soooo, Plan B . . . One of the landowners, Isaac Kenton, sends his own wife to Middlewich's workhouse, having her pretend she's a pauper. The idea was for her to find and destroy any evidence Middlewich had against her husband and his cronies."

"Oh boy," said Izzy quietly. "And the landowners spread a rumor that Middlewich had murdered her."

"Exactly," I said. "The perfect way to make Middlewich look like even more of a despicable lowlife. The trouble was, Mrs. Kenton didn't find the evidence she was searching for. So somehow, the landowners managed to persuade the police to raid the house twice, and *they* didn't find anything either. Why not?"

I paused. Smiles began to creep across the faces of

my audience. Then everyone started nodding knowingly.

"Because," I said triumphantly, "the evidence was hidden behind that wall paneling. *That* was what the secret compartment was for: hiding *this* journal. Middlewich was a smart man. He knew those landowners would be after his blood, so he kept every last piece of evidence here, in his journal, safely tucked away, ready for whenever trouble started brewing."

"Which it did," said Jack.

I nodded. "By then it was 1844. The landowners were up in arms, the police were getting involved, and Middlewich knew that soon the game would be up. He had to pass on his evidence, his journal, his 'dark and mighty treasure,' to someone who could look after it and take to the authorities if necessary."

"Josiah Flagg again," said Muddy.

"Flagg had secretly been on Middlewich's side the whole time," I said. "The landowners didn't suspect him. If Middlewich's journal went to Josiah Flagg, it would be safe. The last few days of Middlewich's life are still a mystery, but obviously he felt that his hiding place, behind the paneling, was no longer safe enough. So in the back of his journal he wrote down those clues. He tore out the page, and put the page behind the paneling instead."

"And it fit into the secret compartment perfectly," said Izzy, "because it was torn from the same notebook the compartment had been designed for in the first place."

"Yes!" I exclaimed. "He buried the journal in the basement."

"And then?" said Muddy.

"And then, the story ends," I said sadly. "The journal was buried, and we have nothing to tell us what happened next. My guess is that the undercover Mrs. Kenton and the mysterious Martha Humble—the woman who killed Middlewich—were one and the same."

"Mrs. Kenton murdered him?" said Jack.

"Now that we know that Middlewich wasn't cruel to the people staying here, as the story goes, it doesn't make sense for him to have been killed by one of his residents. They had no reason to hate him. But Mrs.

Kenton did. Izzy's research revealed that Middlewich's killer said he'd swindled her husband. Well, we now know what she meant."

"But why didn't Josiah Flagg get hold of the journal, as Middlewich intended?" said Jack.

I shrugged. "I guess that's something that will remain a mystery. Maybe he didn't get the chance to follow the trail. Maybe the landowners found out about him. Maybe Middlewich died before he could tell Flagg about the secret compartment. Whatever the truth is, time passed, and Silas Middlewich drifted off into history as a crook and a scoundrel. Well, until now. Until Saxby Smart got on the case!"

"But what if it's the journal that's phony?" said Izzy. "What if Middlewich wrote it just to make people change their minds about him?"

"It's a question of character," I answered. "Remember how I said that the historical accounts of Silas Middlewich didn't match the facts we could deduce about him from the scroll? The whole point of the treasure hunt only makes sense once you realize that Middlewich was a good guy."

"You know," said Jack's dad, "I bet that journal would be worth something to local historians. Hey, it might even pay for a few cans of paint!"

As it turned out, Jack's dad was right and wrong. Right, because the journal certainly did turn out to be of interest to historians. Wrong, because the sale of the journal at auction a few weeks later didn't pay for a few cans of paint. It paid for the entire renovation of the house.

Once everything was sorted out, I returned to my toolshed to write up my notes and sit in my Thinking Chair. The journal is currently on display in a museum. It's strange to think that something that was once so secret is now gawked at every day by kids on school trips. And it's also strange to think that I was able to help a Victorian regain his proper place in history.

Case closed.

CASE FILE SIX:

THE FANGS OF THE DRAGON

CHAPTER ONE

I don't know about you, but I always find it odd when I see my teachers outside of school. It's as if you don't expect them to have a life beyond school doors. In your head, they're always chugging coffee in the teachers' lounge—never filling up shopping carts at the Super-Save.

So I was surprised when, one weekend, Miss Bennett showed up at my toolshed. She teaches the grade below me and runs the book club I go to once a week after school.

As usual, the *Saxby Smart—Private Detective* sign fell off the door the second she knocked, and as usual I found myself apologizing for being unable to nail a simple piece of wood to a door. I tossed the sign into a corner, undecided on whether or not I should use a bigger nail next time or just give up on having a sign altogether. Paint it! I should paint the words on the door! Of course! Why didn't I think of—

Anyway, I let Miss Bennett sit in my Thinking Chair, and I perched on my desk. It was the middle of spring, and the various gardening supplies I'm forced to share my shed with were giving off the aroma of cut grass. I could feel my hay fever coming on.

Miss Bennett is, as far as I can tell, the youngest teacher in school. She's certainly one of the most popular. If the adjective "willowy" didn't exist already, you'd have to invent it specifically for her. She has eyes that look as if they've been borrowed from a cartoon deer, and a mop of frizzy blond hair that's constantly struggling to free itself from the little elastic band holding it in a ponytail. She was the last person I would've expected to bring me one of the weirdest cases I've ever come across.

"How can I help you?" I said. I had my arms in a sort of thinking pose, so as to look properly detective-like and on the ball, brain-wise.

"I'm not sure where to begin," said Miss Bennett. "I mentioned this problem in the teachers' lounge, and

several teachers suggested I come and talk to you."

"I see." I wasn't sure whether it was a good thing to be talked about in the teachers' lounge. "So, what kind of problem is this? Has a crime been committed?"

"Well . . ." said Miss Bennett, her face taking on a sort of er-um-I-dunno expression, "more like a sort of non-crime, really. In fact, a whole series of non-crimes."

"You've come to see a private eye about a crime not being committed?" I said.

"It's like this," she explained. "Over the past few weeks, six of my students have had intruders in their homes."

"Ah! So each house has been broken into?"

"Noooooo. There's been no sign of forced entry."

"Ah! So stuff's been stolen?"

"Noooooo. Well, some cash has gone missing. But there could be other explanations for that."

"Ah! So burglars have been caught in the act, before they could escape?"

"Noooooo. Nobody's been seen."

"So . . ." I said, my eyes narrowing. "Let's recap. Six of your students have not had break-ins, have had nothing stolen, and have not spotted any sketchy-looking guys lurking in the bushes. Hmm, yes, I can see that they'd be worried."

"I know it sounds crazy, Saxby, but each of these six is convinced that *someone* has been in their house."

Now it was my turn to use the er-um-I-dunno expression. "Why?"

"That's half the problem," said Miss Bennett. "There's nothing they can be sure of. It's a feeling. They're positive that things have been moved, ever so slightly. Objects examined, closets opened, desks rifled through. Things like that."

"Couldn't they just be, I dunno, oversensitive or something?"

"I might think that too, but *six* of them? In the same class? Within a few weeks? That seems very odd. And none of them is the type of kid who makes stuff up."

"Hmm, yes, I see your point. But couldn't it also be a case of one person saying something, and the others picking up on it?"

"No," said Miss Bennett. "This only came to light because we were having a class discussion the other day. One of the girls, Sarah, happened to mention this strange feeling she and her mom recently had, and then the five others spoke up and said they'd experienced exactly the same thing. None of them had mentioned it before, because at the time they all thought, as you would have, that it was nothing more than an isolated oddity."

"You said that money's been stolen?" I asked.

"Yes, four of these six say that they or their parents have had small amounts of money go missing. A ten-dollar bill, or some loose change they thought they'd left in a particular spot. Again, nothing that's really definite. With no break-ins and nothing else taken, they all thought they'd simply misplaced the money. But now, because this has happened six times, the missing money suddenly looks like a sign of deliberate theft."

"It certainly does," I said. "But what kind of thief leaves no trace of breaking in, takes nothing but small amounts of money, and only takes money four times out of six?"

"Precisely," said Miss Bennett. "*Now* do you see why I came to you? My whole class is really worried about this, and so am I. We're all wondering who's next."

"Haven't any of their parents gone to the police?"

"And tell them what?" said Miss Bennett. "There's still no actual evidence of any crime being committed. What could the police do?"

"Good point," I said. I hopped off the desk and onto my feet. "Well, I can honestly say that this is the weirdest problem anyone's ever come to me with. Ever."

"So . . . you don't think it can be investigated?" asked Miss Bennett.

"On the contrary," I said. I tried to sound confident, but to be perfectly honest, I didn't feel the least bit confident at all. This case seemed totally baffling, even before it had begun! However:

"I've yet to turn down a genuine mystery," I said, "and I don't intend to start now. Saxby Smart is on the case!"

FACT: Six households, six no-break-ins, six no-crimes-except-possibly-some-cash-being-taken. And yet, firm impressions all around that an intruder had been at work.

POSSIBILITY 1: They've all gone a little nuts. Convenient—all I'd have to do is say, "You've gone a little nuts," and case closed—but not very likely.

POSSIBILITY 2: We've got a burglar who walks through walls and doesn't like stealing things all that much. Not. Very. Likely.

CONNECTION: All these incidents have happened within a small group of people—one class. So! There's a probable link between the incidents and the school. Must investigate further.

PROBLEM: However, that doesn't change the basic problem here, which is that—so far—the only evidence we have that these incidents took place at all are the gut reactions of those involved!

So! All I've got to go on are feelings. And feelings are not facts. I need facts. Not feelings. Facts. And there are none to go on. Plus, I think my hay fever is really starting to kick in. I am not happy.

CHAPTER TWO

When you're a brilliant detective like me, you can't afford to let anything pass you by. You never know when a clue or a connection or a significant fact could turn up and blow a case wide open. You must always be on the lookout. Always.

On Monday morning, I was about as on the lookout as a dead possum. The pollen count was at an all-time high, and my nose was at an all-time low. I slouched to school, cursing my parents' DNA for passing on the hay fever gene to their only child! I couldn't decide which were runnier, my eyes or my nostrils. I was not in the best condition to observe and deduce.

Even so, taking my usual route across the park at 8:40 a.m., I noticed something very strange. If you've read my previous volume of case files, you're well aware of that low-down rat, Harry Lovecraft. He's in my class, but, as I like to say, the rest of us out-class him in every way, ha ha. Harry Lovecraft is my arch-enemy, a sneaky, smarmy, shiny-haired weasel who's about as trustworthy as a starving cobra in a box full of white mice. If there's a dirty trick to be played in the playground, he'll play it.

So I was naturally suspicious when I saw him taking his usual route across the park, chatting amiably to a group of younger kids. Believe me, that low-down rat Harry Lovecraft never chats amiably to anyone, least of all kids in the grades below him. Tricks them out of their lunch money, yes, but chats amiably, no.

I walked faster and caught up with the group. They seemed to be talking about wizards, frog people, and something called a "Grand Croak Toad Belcher."

"What are you ubb to, Lovecraft?" I said.

"Deary me, Smart," oozed Harry Lovecraft, "is that allergies, or has someone finally given you the smack in the face you deserve?"

The kids around him giggled. Some of them were from Miss Bennett's homeroom, and the rest from the other class in that grade.

I tried to think of a witty comeback. I couldn't. "Just shudd ubb, Lovecraft," I said. "You're ubb to something."

"We're talking about FrogWar BattleZone," piped up one of the kids. "You collect the figures and paint them. We're all making our own battleboards."

I glared at Harry Lovecraft as best I could with my bloodshot, pollen-bloated eyes. "You're never into FrogWar," I said. "Whadd sneaky liddle plot are you haddching now?"

Harry Lovecraft took a step closer to me. Clipped to his jacket was the latest mini MP3 player, a model that had only hit stores about a week ago.

"That's the trouble with busybodies like you,

Smart," he said and then sneered. "You always think the worst of people."

"No, not peeble in general," I sneered back. "Just you."

I turned to leave. Or rather, to carry on walking ahead of them. I'd only gone a few steps when I turned back with a question for Harry.

"Your birthday's not for three more muddths, is it?" I said.

"What?" blinked Harry, confused. "Planning a surprise party for me, are you?"

I walked on. Despite having a sneezing fit that lasted all the way to school, I was secretly congratulating myself. I now had *two* reasons for thinking that Harry Lovecraft might somehow be involved in these mysterious non-break-ins I was investigating—two coincidences that made me suspicious.

Have you spotted them?

The two coincidences were:

1. Harry Lovecraft's little FrogWar group included a number of Miss Bennett's students. Under normal conditions, he'd *never* be nice to those kids. Was there a link between his sudden interest and the non-break-ins experienced by Miss Bennett's class?

2. Some money had—probably, apparently— gone missing. And Harry Lovecraft suddenly owned an MP3 player he couldn't have bought earlier than last week, when it came out. From past experience, I knew he was enough of a low-down rat to resort to petty theft.

The problem was, *how* could Harry Lovecraft be linked to these "un-crimes"? As far as I knew, he hadn't suddenly gained the ability to walk through walls (which this phantom-like burglar seemed to be doing).

On the *plus* side: these un-crimes clearly showed a great deal of careful sneakiness—a classic Lovecraft trademark!

BUT! On the *minus* side: being so careful and

sneaky seemed like sort of a waste, if all that got swiped was some cash. If Harry Lovecraft wanted cash, he usually just pulled another lunch-money scam.

BUT! On the *plus* side: news of another lunch-money scam hadn't reached me all semester. So Harry Lovecraft's sudden flaunting of new goods made a link with the un-crimes all the more likely.

BUT! On the *minus* side: would even that low-down rat turn to actual burglary? I'd never seen him go *that* far, ever.

By the time I reached school, not only was my nose gunked up with snot, but my brain was gunked up with a jumble of confusing and contradictory thoughts. Before attendance sign-in, I hurried over to Miss Bennett's class and asked that the six victims of the un-crimes stay behind at recess.

There were three items on my To Do list:

- Talk to these six, and find out more about each individual incident.
- Keep a close eye on H. Lovecraft.
- Get hold of more tissues. The ones I'd brought from home were already reduced to damp shreds.

While our homeroom teacher, Mrs. Penzler, was handing out exercises for the first lesson of the day, I leaned across to the desk beside me and had a quiet word with my friend George "Muddy" Whitehouse, as follows:

Me: (checking that neither Mrs. Penzler nor H. Lovecraft was looking my way) Muddy, I'm going to be busy with a case during recess. Can you keep a close eye on Harry Lovecraft for me?

Muddy: Will do! Awesome! I've got some home-made spy gear with me.

Me: Why do you have to keep bringing spies into everything?

Muddy: Spies are cool.

Me: So are fridges, so what? We are not spies. This is detective work.

Muddy: (making a face) . . . It's kind of like being spies.

Me: No, it's not, it's—(waving hands around). Just forget about spies. Watch Harry Lovecraft. Don't let him know you're keeping tabs on him, okay? Be casual. Be subtle.

Muddy: Casual and subtle, check. (Pause) The seagulls fly south over Moscow.

Me: . . . What?

Muddy: It's what spies say.

Me: Oh, shut up.

Mrs. Penzler: Saxby, less chatter please!

Me: Sorry!

The second the bell rang for recess, I zipped over to Miss Bennett's classroom. I talked to each of the six one by one, and made careful notes. Here are the results:

INCIDENT 1

Student's name: Maggie Hamilton

Date/time/location: April 24th/between 10 a.m. and 1 p.m./14 Meadow Road

What happened: Maggie's mom came home, thought several things had been moved—computer keyboard, address book by kitchen phone, pile of bills; $20 on front-hall table gone. Mom has large jewelry box in bedroom—untouched.

Any other relevant info: Mom and Dad think Mom's just mistaken (neighbor says she saw Mom get home at 11:30 a.m., Mom thought she hadn't returned until 1 p.m.); Dad was away on business all that week;

Mom works afternoons at the SuperSave.

INCIDENT 2

Student's name: Patrick Atwood

Date/time/location: May 1st/in the morning, "sometime after 10:15"/26 Avon Street

What happened: Files and papers on desk disturbed; drawers rifled through.

Any Other Relevant Info: Patrick's mom works from home—this happened on the only day of the week she's not there; very worried that "intruder" knew this and/or was watching the house.

INCIDENT 3

Student's name: Sarah Hardy (she was the one who'd first mentioned the "un-crimes" in class)

Date/time/location: May 8th/"must've been between 9:45 and noon"/Park Court, Apartment 2

What happened: Stuff around computer moved; trash basket in living room "in wrong position"; pile of change on hallway bookshelf gone; $10 bill from Mom's bureau gone (credit cards untouched).

Any other relevant info: Mom thinks Sarah's

two older sisters stole the money; sisters grounded; sisters not happy. Only Sarah noticed the other items being moved—sisters distracted by high school classes, Mom distracted by daily hobby of shopping(!); Mom calls Sarah's suggestion of an intruder "ridiculous."

INCIDENT 4

Student's name: Thomas Waters

Date/time/location: May 15th/"sometime late morning"/36 Field Lane

What happened: Drawers left slightly open; box of old paperwork disturbed; kitchen trash can moved; $20 in singles and change gone from teakettle in kitchen(?!), but Mom has convinced herself she used this money for Chinese takeout the week before.

Any other relevant info: Thomas's mom suspicious when returned home from appointment; Thomas's dad always at work from 7 a.m. to 7 p.m.; Mom works with Maggie Hamilton's mom at the SuperSave in the afternoons and is friends with Liz Wyndham's mom down the street.

INCIDENT 5

Student's name: Liz Wyndham

Date/time/location: May 22nd / before 12 p.m. / 45 Field Lane

What happened: Work desk disturbed; angle of computer screen changed; closets searched through.

Any other relevant info: Liz's mom works part-time from home—only leaves house a couple of times a week due to medical stuff; Liz asked nosy Mrs. Huxley from across the street if she'd seen anything that day ("she misses *nothing*")—Mrs. H. claimed Liz's mom left house at 9:20 a.m., came back at 10:50 a.m., left again at 11:05 a.m., and returned home again at 12! But Liz's mom says she was out all morning, from 9:20 on. Liz is worried about her mom!

INCIDENT 6

Student's name: John Wurtzel

Date/time/location: May 29th /"had to be between 10:15 and 11:45 a.m." / 177 Deadman's Lane

What happened: Cupboard door in dining room ajar; laptop closed when it had been open; bills pinned to bulletin board slightly moved; glass bowl on mantelpiece emptied of loose change.

Any other relevant info: John's parents are divorced—Dad is an office manager, Mom is an artist who spends almost all day every day in her studio in the attic. Mom thinks Dad turned up and moved stuff around just to confuse and annoy her(!).

Looking through these notes on the way back to my class, *lots* of interesting links and possibilities jumped out at me faster than a pouncing tiger. Links involving dates, times, even the nature of the incidents themselves.

I could see three remarkable coincidences, one really weird connection, and—arg!—something that more or less proved Harry Lovecraft could *not* be the intruder.

How many of your conclusions match mine?

ITEM 1—three remarkable coincidences:

1. **The timing of each incident.** In every case, it happened on a *Thursday* (the dates are seven days apart)! And on a Thursday *morning*, too, between about a quarter to ten and one o'clock!

2. **The families involved.** In every case, there was *no dad* around at the time of the incident—every dad was either away or at work, or absent for some other reason. *And*, building on that: it struck me as very odd that all six of these moms were people who just happened to be free on those Thursday mornings. They were self-employed, or they worked in the afternoons, or whatever. They were all people who, on those Thursday mornings, could arrange their own schedules.

3. **The stuff that was disturbed.** Strangely similar in each case—household papers, stuff in drawers, and computers in particular. This simply *had* to be significant!

ITEM 2—one really weird connection:

In two cases out of the six, somebody saw the relevant mom at home at a time when the mom claimed to have been out. Maggie Hamilton's mom and Liz Wyndham's mom were both spotted by neighbors.

Now, if that had happened in *one* case, I'd have written it off as a simple mistake. Someone got their time wrong. But it happened *twice*, and it happened twice within this very specific, already coincidence-packed group of six. Now *that's* weird!

ITEM 3—Harry Lovecraft now had a perfect alibi:

Thursday mornings, he was at school.

Hmm . . .

On my way back to class, my sinuses a bit better now that I'd been away from fresh air for a while, Muddy gave me a full report on what that low-down rat Harry Lovecraft had been up to during recess. The report was pretty much exactly what I'd expected.

"He's been talking to different kids from the grade below," whispered Muddy, as everyone filed back into the classroom, "and some in the grade below *that* too."

"Good work," I whispered.

"There was a lot of chitchat about giant frogs or something, I didn't really follow that part. But I think that was just a cover. What he was really trying to find out was personal details. What their parents do for a living, what part of town they live in, that sort of thing."

"Excellent work," I whispered. "I assume these kids didn't suspect him of anything?"

"No," whispered Muddy. "They think they've got some great new friend. He keeps claiming he can get them a discount on those frog thingies."

"*Brilliant* work," I whispered. "How did you get all that info? Careful eavesdropping and deduction?"

"No, I went up to them and asked."

"You did *what*?" I cried. Some of our classmates turned in our direction. "I told you to be casual and subtle!"

"You told me to not use my spy gear!" protested Muddy. "I had the Whitehouse Listen-O-Phone 2000 in my bag, but oooh nooo, not allowed. I don't have

super-power hearing, you know! I can't listen in from
the other side of the playground!"

"Now Harry's going to know we're investigating
him," I hissed.

"Tut tut," said a voice behind us, a voice that was
slimier than a snail's handshake. That low-down rat
Harry Lovecraft swanned past us, grinning his sick
grin. "Tut tut, Smart; is one of your trained poodles
not doing his tricks?"

Muddy made a remark about tricks and trained
poodles that can't be repeated in these pages. From
the other side of the classroom, Mrs. Penzler clacked a
ruler on her desk for attention.

"Is there a problem? Saxby Smart? George Whitehouse?"

"Sorry!" I cried.

More important thoughts sparked by the Harry Lovecraft connection, and from my investigations so far:

Obviously, nobody's walking through walls here. The intruder is either using actual keys, or is an incredible lock picker. As of now, there are no leads whatsoever on this point. The intruder has clearly made quite an effort to get in, yet has taken very little. <u>Why?</u> It must have something to do with whatever items were disturbed.

VITAL QUESTION: What is this intruder really looking for? And what is going on with those two moms who were seen at home when they said they <u>weren't</u> at home? To have the <u>intruder</u> seen at those times would make sense, but those neighbors positively identified the moms, <u>not</u> a stranger.

CONCLUSION: Huh???

IMPORTANT POINT: I have no reason to think the intruder will stop at six break-ins. Who's next?

All of this leads to a specific question: I need to know <u>exactly</u> what the six moms were doing when they were out on each "incident" day!

CHAPTER THREE

Before the end of the day, I asked the six affected students in Miss Bennett's class the specific question my notes had led me to. The following morning, I had six specific answers.

Maggie Hamilton: "She left at ten, drove to the post office, then she was at something called Monsieur Jacques's De-Stress Session from 10:30 to 11:30. Then she drove into town for lunch with my grandma, then home at one o'clock."

Patrick Atwood: "At 10:15 she walked to her weekly de-stress session, which is run by some French guy from Dragonfang Gym. After that she did some shopping at the SuperSave, then came home."

Sarah Hardy: "After leaving the house, she stopped

in at the dentist's to make an appointment, then she was at Monsieur Jacques's class until 11:30, then she came straight back."

Thomas Waters: "She says the only place she went to was her regular de-stress class. I said to her, 'De-stress? More like distress,' because she's so wound-up you'd think she was clockwork. And she said to me, 'Stop being a brat and set the table'. . ." etc., etc.

Liz Wyndham: "Mom went to the doctor's at 9:45. After that, she went to a weekly thing run by Dragon-fang Gym. Then back home around noon."

John Wurtzel: "She's got it all on her calendar, apparently. Quarter past ten, leaves the house to go to her stress-free meeting, or something like that. Then back home and in her studio the rest of the day."

"Bingo," I said quietly to myself, smiling a huge smile. Then I stopped smiling and said, "Uh-oh!" not at all quietly.

It was a Tuesday. On Thursday there would be another one of those Monsieur Jacques classes. At which time, someone, somewhere, was going to get a visit . . .

I had two days to track down the intruder!

Think, think, think! I told myself. Find out whose moms would be attending Thursday's class. That would give me all the addresses of where the intruder might strike next. But how could I know which address would be next on the list?

There was only one way to proceed: get as much information as possible on this Monsieur Jacques and Dragonfang Gym. During lunch, while everyone was chewing on cardboardlike piecrusts and trying to hide their uneaten peas from the lunch ladies, I talked to my friend Izzy. As those who've examined my earlier case files will know, Isobel Moustique is St. Egbert's number one genius, and quite possibly the girliest girl on the face of the planet. I filled her in on the story thus far as I struggled to cut into my piece of pie.

"So," I said, gritting my teeth as I leaned as heavily as I dared on my knife and fork, "I need all the background info you can give me on both the gym and the French guy."

"No problem," she said. "This Monsieur Jacques person has only been in the fitness industry for a few months, but he's already built up quite a large list of clients. He has all his classes in people's homes— yoga, weight training, relaxation, the usual thing. Each member of the class takes a turn to host a session. Like I said, he hasn't been at it long, but he's already planning on closing Dragonfang Gym at the end of the year. Apparently, he and his wife are moving to Africa to do charity work."

"You're amazing," I gasped, open-mouthed. "I simply name a topic, and you know all about it! Incredible!"

"Noooot really," said Izzy, making a you-poor-dumb-fool face. "My mom just signed up for one of his classes."

"Aha," I said quickly. "Yes, I thought so, of course." I shoveled some peas onto my fork. They fell off.

"And before you ask," said Izzy, "no, my mom's class is not on a Thursday morning. It's tonight at six."

"That's perfect," I said. "Could she get me in there? I want to observe this Monsieur Jacques up close."

"I don't think they normally let kids into these sessions," said Izzy, "but I'm sure we can think of something."

I chewed my way through a particularly tough section of pastry. "Aren't you having the pie?" I said.

She gave my plate one of her arch, feline looks. "As if," she said. She unzipped her pink sandwich bag and took out a container of homemade pasta salad and a fork.

CHAPTER FOUR

Have you ever noticed how some family members seem almost identical, while the members of other families seem about as alike as a jar of jelly and the Empire State Building?

Izzy's mom was as unlike her daughter as two people could possibly be without major genetic re-sequencing. Whereas Isobel was all glitzy clothes and chunky rings, her mother was somber and businesslike.

At six o'clock that evening, as we stood together on the doorstep of 29 Mercia Way, Izzy's mom looked ready to march into a high-powered, top-level executive meeting and start firing people. And that's not an easy look to achieve in a track suit. I still had on my school clothes.

The door was opened by the owner of the house,

Mrs. Ferguson. It was her turn to host this week's session.

"Hello, hello," she twittered, ushering us inside. "Lovely to see you, Caroline. Who's this with you?"

I'd given Izzy's mom my carefully thought-out cover story. I was to be Matt, her adopted nephew. I was to be staying with her while my house was getting repaired after a gas explosion. I was to be accompanying her this evening due to the traumatic after-effects of having my house blown up.

"This," said Izzy's mom, "is my daughter's friend Saxby. He's just tagging along."

"Nice to meet you," said Mrs. Ferguson. "The more the merrier; please come right in, Monsieur Jacques has arrived and we're ready to start."

As we walked into the living room, I nudged Izzy's mom in the ribs.

"What about my carefully thought-out cover story?" I whispered.

"Don't be silly," said Izzy's mom. "Half the people here will know you from school. What on earth do you need a cover story for?"

"It's more detective-like," I grumbled.

Assembled in the living room were a dozen other women in track suits. Standing in front of them was a man with an elaborate hairdo shaped like a headless duck, and a mustache that set a whole new standard for the phrase "thin and weedy." He wore bright yellow pants and a polo-style T-shirt with Dragonfang printed across the chest. A gold badge with a dragon logo was pinned above the letters.

So this was Monsieur Jacques. Immediately, his face seemed vaguely familiar to me.

"Good evening, everyone," he cried, clapping politely for quiet. (For the full effect here, you need to imagine his words in a French accent as thick as week-old gravy.) "To business! *Voilà!* We 'ave ze beginning exercise! Aaaaand . . . "

Everyone lined up and started sticking their legs out at weird angles. I nudged Izzy's mom again.

"I forgot to ask," I whispered. "Which class is this, exactly? Advanced Relaxation? Meditation for Beginners?"

"Ballet-robics," said Izzy's mom. "Come on, get those arms moving."

Thumpy music started up on the CD player. If my heart had sunk any lower, I'd have been standing on it. "Great," I muttered.

I reminded myself that I was here to make careful observations. I was still troubled by the fact that Monsieur Jacques seemed strangely familiar. And I was even more troubled by his accent. Something, as Monsieur Jacques would probably say, smelled of ze fish.

"That's it, *mes amis*!" cried Monsieur Jacques. "Kick and twirl! And one, two, three; one, two, three! That is good, Mrs. Ferguson! Also good, Mrs. Moustique!"

After a few minutes, he shut up a bit and started patrolling each of his students, tapping out the rhythm of the music with his fingers. I took the chance to ask him some deceptively innocent questions. The first of these questions was based on a snippet of historical knowledge I'd collected during the case of *The Trea-sure of Dead Man's Lane* . . .

"This is a really wonderful class, Monsieur Jacques," I said, above the music's beat. "Absolutely outstand-ing."

He glanced at me as though I was something he'd recently picked from his nose. "*Merci*," he said. "Aaaand one, two—"

"Why did you name your gym Dragonfang?" I said. "Why not something more French; maybe something historical, like 'Waterloo.' You know, to commemorate Napoleon's victory?"

He tapped his gold dragon badge. "Yes, of course I considered 'Waterloo,' but I am ze, as you say, fan of ze martial arts movies. My favorite, it eez *Dragon War-rior Goes Nuts in Shanghai*. You know it?"

"*Oui!* Or, as it translates into French, *Le Penzler de Bennett Izzy de la Muddi*, right?"

"*Oui*, exactly," he said. "Now then, come along, one, two—"

"But I hear you're closing the gym soon?" I said, putting on my best sorrowful-puppy-dog expression.

"Yes," said Monsieur Jacques, "ze Mrs. Wife and I,

we do ze work for ze charity in Africa; we 'elp orphans build ze shelters for endangered species in ze Brazilian rainforest. Soon we sell up and move there." He clapped his hands and raised his voice. "In time with ze music! Good! Lovely work, everyone! Three, four, five . . . "

I knew it! The guy was a total fake, no more French than my Aunt Pat. And I doubted he could even point to Africa on a map of nothing but Africa, with Africa circled in red, and a sign saying *Africa, This Way* taped on top of it!

Did you catch his three mistakes?

1. Napoleon LOST the Battle of Waterloo. (For more info, see my previous case file.)

2. That translation I gave him was total gibberish. Even I speak more French than him, and all I can manage is ordering a baguette!

3. The Brazilian rain forest is in South America. In, like, you know, um, Brazil! It's nowhere near Africa.

I tapped Monsieur Jacques's sleeve. "Could I ask if you—?"

He was clearly getting ever so slightly fed up with my questions. "I don't appear to 'ave your name on my list, young man. 'Ave you paid for ze session?"

"Er, no, I'm just tagging along," I said.

"Well, tag along to ze kitchen and make ze tea," said Monsieur Jacques. He gave me a smarmy smile.

And in that instant, I knew why his face looked familiar. Remember what I said about family resemblances? Monsieur Jacques's smarmy smile was identical to the smarmy smile of a certain low-down rat from school . . .

My heart suddenly started to race. So as to not give anything away to "Monsieur Jacques," I quickly retreated to the kitchen. While the kettle boiled, I called Izzy.

"Stand by," I said. "I'll get a picture of him and send it to you right away."

"Okie-dokie," she said.

I hurried back into the living room, holding the phone to my ear as if Izzy was still on the line. I planned to stand as close to our phony French friend as I could, pretend to be deep in conversation, and click the camera button when he wasn't looking.

The living room was empty.

For a second or two I panicked, thinking that the class was suddenly over and that everyone had gone home. But as the steady throb of the music continued, I could hear people moving around all over the house.

Two members of the class reappeared, and kick-stepped their way across the room. I spotted a couple more of them twirling and stretching in the hallway. From somewhere upstairs came a familiar, honey-coated accent: "Looovely, Mrs. Ferguson, hold your

leg in zat position and spin! Yeeees, that is perfecto; you three there, please to be going downstairs to join ze group in ze dining room. Loooovely!"

I found Izzy's mom doing funny-looking arm movements on the stairs.

"Does every class include this different-rooms routine?" I asked.

"Oh yes," said Izzy's mom, continuing to wave her arms around like a slow-motion windmill. "We always split up, spread out, and move around. Monsieur Jacques says it's to give us a free-flowing feeling of personal space. He says it allows him to assess us individually."

A crime-related thought popped into my mind. "Yes," I said, "and I bet that's not all it allows him to do."

Monsieur Jacques appeared at the top of the staircase and started lightly skipping down the steps toward us. "Mrs. Ferguson," he called back over his shoulder, "ze spinning, she is enough now, you will get dizzy again."

As he drew level with Izzy's mom and me, he smiled at one of us and sneered at the other. I'll leave you to guess which of us got the sneer.

"You 'ave made ze tea?" he said.

"Oui," I replied. "Ze kettle, she is boiled."

For the briefest of split seconds, the look on his face said, "I don't like you, sunshine!" But then he switched his attention to Izzy's mom, grinning sappily at her. He dug into his pocket and produced a gold badge like the one he wore, with a dragon logo printed on it.

"Mrs. Moustique!" he declared. "You 'ave made such terrific effort this evening. You are quite a new member to our group, but already I award you my Star Student badge!"

"Oh, thank you very much," said Izzy's mom, as he pinned it to her track suit. There was a ripple of applause from upstairs.

I took the opportunity, while Monsieur Jacques's attention was diverted, to flip open my phone. I got an excellent shot of his face while he was busy asking Izzy's mom for her monthly membership fee.

Later, after I'd sent the picture to Izzy and was back home, I waited nervously for confirmation of the evening's findings. I didn't have to wait very long. Izzy called me back within the hour.

"You were right to suggest I look back through crime reports on news sites," she said. "It didn't take me long to find this Monsieur Jacques. The pictures I've got of him are ten years old, but it's definitely the same guy."

"Ten years old?" I said. "Why's that?"

"Because until the middle of last year, he was in prison," said Izzy. "He ran a gang that conned half a million bucks out of some Third World charity groups. What a jerk!"

"And his real name?"

"Oh yeah, that's the best part," said Izzy. "You were totally right. He certainly isn't French. His name is Jack Lovecraft. He's Harry's uncle."

That piece of information was the last piece in the puzzle. I now knew exactly what had been going on. I knew what those non-break-ins were all about, and I knew what Harry had been up to.

But catching the intruder would still be difficult.

CHAPTER FIVE

Thursday, 10:55 a.m.

"Can't we park outside the house?" asked Miss Bennett.

"No!" I cried. "We can't be seen, we can't let the intruder suspect anything."

Miss Bennett stopped the school van, and we all got out: Miss Bennett, me, the six students in Miss Bennett's class who'd already been visited by the intruder, and a seventh student, a scruffy boy named Oliver.

"I live at the other end of the street," said Oliver, as Miss Bennett locked up the van.

"Exactly," I said. "That's why we're here. Okay, everyone, most of these houses have hedges around their front yards. Keep down, below the bushes, out of sight."

Everyone crouched down and shuffled along the street toward Oliver's house. An old lady walking a tiny dog passed us on the other side of the road. Both of them gave us a funny look.

"Honestly, Saxby," said Miss Bennett crossly, "is this really necessary?"

"It's vital," I whispered.

"Why couldn't you have talked to us at school?" said Miss Bennett.

"Because until we've caught the intruder red-handed, news can't get out at school that the mystery's been solved. One sneaky phone call from Harry Love-craft, and the intruder will bail on the whole scheme and make a run for it. I've got Muddy covering for me

back in class. As far as Harry's concerned, I'm at the optician's getting my glasses adjusted."

"You're making some pretty serious allegations about that boy," said Miss Bennett quietly. "You'd better have your facts straight."

By now, we'd reached Oliver's house. Luckily, the bushes around his yard were particularly tall and thick. We all scrunched down, at a point where we couldn't be seen from the front door or any of the windows.

I checked my watch. 11 a.m. precisely.

"Okay," I said. "Now, we all know that right at this moment there's a weekly de-stress session going on, which the mothers of all seven of you are attending. This week, it's over at Liz Wyndham's house."

"Right," said Liz Wyndham.

"The homes of six members of that class have already been visited by a mysterious intruder," I said. "Oliver here is the only person we know of whose mom is at that class but whose home has *not* yet been visited by a mysterious intruder."

"Wait a minute," said Miss Bennett. "Surely there are more than seven people at this session? How can we know which house is next on the intruder's list?"

"Welllllllll," I said, "strictly speaking, we can't . . . "

"So we could all be crouching here behind a bush, like a bunch of idiots, using up class time, for nothing?" said Miss Bennett.

"Strictly speaking . . . yes," I admitted. "But I have every reason to believe I'm right, and that the intruder is right now, as we speak, in Oliver's house."

"Well, let's get in there and grab him, then!" cried Oliver.

"Shhh!" I hissed. "No good. If we barge in there, the intruder could simply dump the evidence we need and run out the back door. We have to wait. We have to catch them."

"But what's this evidence you're talking about?" said Miss Bennett. "And how *do* you know this is the right house?"

"Look at what we know so far," I said. "In every case, the intruder has struck at a house they *know* will be empty. Think about it from the intruder's point of view. Mom X attends a gym class. So *she's* out of the house, but half a dozen *more* people might still be at home! An intruder will want to minimize the risk of finding the place still occupied. *That* is the link between all seven of you here. All seven of you can confirm to a third party that, on a Thursday morning, when Mom's at her gym class, there's nobody else at home."

"A third party?" said Oliver.

"You mean . . . Harry Lovecraft?" said Miss Bennett.

"Exactly!" I said. "He's been unusually friendly lately. He's been chatting away with people left and right. And the interest he takes in all his new friends covers up the fact that he's fishing for information. About your moms and dads, about what goes on at home . . . "

"That stupid, slimy, double-crossing . . . " muttered Liz Wyndham.

"So," said Miss Bennett, "cross-referencing the addresses of the people who attend the gym class, with the information gathered by Harry, means that the intruder can know which houses would make for the best targets."

"Exactly," I said. "Of course, the intruder only *needs* to have an address, and can use various tricks to find out if there's someone else at home, but the information provided by Harry would be a perfect shortcut to targeting houses left unattended."

"But we're still no closer to knowing *how* or *why* these things are happening," said Miss Bennett. "The intruder can't be the man running the classes. He's running the classes."

"How is Monsieur Jacques involved?" said Liz Wyndham. "My mom thinks the world of him."

"I'm afraid Monsieur Jacques is really Monsieur Harry Lovecraft's uncle, a man with a criminal record as long as an anteater's tongue. He got out of prison last year, set up Dragonfang Gym, and is using it as a front for his latest con act."

"You mean he's holding all these classes as a kind of distraction, so that the intruder can get to work?" said Miss Bennett.

"Oh, he's doing a lot more than that," I said. "Remember how there's never any sign of an actual break-in? That's because the intruder is using a key. You see, because Monsieur Jacques has his classes in people's homes, he's got every opportunity to snoop. He sends people off around the house, doing their exercises, and all he needs are a few seconds to locate the owner's key ring, and take an impression of the keys with a bar of soap or a block of modeling clay."

"But if he's going to all that trouble," said Miss Bennett, "why is so little being taken?"

"On the contrary," I said. "A great deal is being taken. Look at the types of things that were disturbed each time. Computers, bills, even trash cans. The intruder is stealing words and numbers."

"Words and numbers?" said Oliver.

"Bank account numbers, computer passwords, login details, financial records. Personal information of all kinds. Identity theft."

"But none of the parents' bank accounts have been emptied or anything like that," said Miss Bennett. "Surely he's not simply stocking up on all that information?"

"Yes, that's precisely what he's doing," I said. "He's already told everyone that he's closing Dragonfang Gym and moving abroad. Not to Africa, as he claims, I'm sure. But somewhere. And when he's safe on the other side of the world, he can use all that info to whatever criminal ends he likes. It's all done by computer. He could be on Mars and still launch raids on one bank account after another."

"Of course," said Miss Bennett, "if he's in another country, it'll be that much harder to trace him, and that much harder for the law to catch up with him."

"Exactly," I said. "He's been running tons of different classes, so by now he's probably got passwords and account numbers for dozens of people, possibly hundreds."

"If that's true," said Liz Wyndham, "why haven't more people in more gym classes noticed these intrusions?"

"Why would they? You guys only noticed by accident. If the intruder is careful enough, most of this scheme's victims won't even realize the intruder visited them."

"Why steal the money?" said Liz Wyndham. "Won't that look suspicious?"

"A little bonus for Harry?" I said. "For services rendered? If Harry wasn't so flashy with his spending, I might not have noticed! In most cases, for most classes, Monsieur Jacques will have had to spend time cozying up to his customers to find out the sorts of household details the intruder would benefit from. But once he realized that several members of this one particular Thursday morning de-stress class were moms at St. Egbert's, he spotted an opportunity. He had a nephew he could use as an inside man!"

"So *who* is in my house, then?" wailed Oliver. "Who is this intruder?"

I was about to answer him when two things happened. First, the front door of Oliver's house swung open. Second, I felt a distinct and sudden itch in my nose. I glanced at the hedge: it was one of those flowering types. I'd been crouching down with my head in an air current loaded with pollen.

"Ohhh, wonbberful!" I sighed.

But I had no time to feel sorry for myself. The door of Oliver's house was standing ajar. So far, no movement came from inside.

Nobody dared to breathe. We all stared through the tiny gaps in the hedge, between the leaves, watching the front door.

11:04 a.m.

Suddenly, moving swiftly, a figure emerged. A woman. She was wearing a long red coat and chunky boots, and a cascade of blond hair fell around her shoulders. She was facing into the house, away from us, as if making sure she hadn't forgotten anything. The upper part of her was deep in the slab of shadow thrown by the balcony that jutted out above the door.

"Nobobby bake a sound," I whispered. "She bite rubb away before we cabb get her."

"Who is she?" whispered Miss Bennett.

Oliver made a slight whimpering noise. "I don't believe it. That's my mom. My mom is the intruder."

The woman shut the front door behind her with a

clunk. She took a key from the pocket of her coat and double-locked the door, giving it a rattle to make sure it was firmly closed.

"So your mom's been the intruder all along?" gasped Liz Wyndham.

"Hold on a sec," whispered Oliver. "This is her own house . . . "

"Be quiedd," I breathed. "She can't . . . know . . . we're . . . AHHHH-CHOOOO!" My sneeze was so loud it sent a flock of sparrows into a panic at the other end of the street.

The woman spun around instantly. Spooked, she made a dash for the gate at the side of the yard.

We all leaped from our hiding place. Miss Bennett, with that willowy frame of hers, would have made a good athlete. She caught up with the woman in less than a dozen loping strides, grabbing her by the shoulders.

The woman cried out angrily. As she tried to wriggle free of Miss Bennett's grip, she lost her balance and toppled onto the lawn.

Her long blond hair had come loose while she fell. The wig dropped to the grass, revealing a short, dark haircut underneath.

"What?!" cried Oliver, from the back of the group. "My mom wears a . . . Hey!"

"I thingg you'll find your bubb is safe at her gybb class," I said, accepting some tissues from Liz Wyndham. "Say hello to Uncle Jack's wife, Harry Lovecraft's aunt Sharon."

Miss Bennett had her securely pinned on the grass. Aunt Sharon glared up at us, a mixture of anger and defiance on her face.

"But why was she disguised as my mom?" said Oliver. "How does she even know what my mom looks like?"

I blew my nose a couple of times. "I told you, Harry's uncle, Monsieur Jacques, has been busy snooping around all your houses whenever he held a class there," I said. "Along with copying keys, he also looked in closets. His wife here, the intruder, could then get hold of similar clothes and hair, and disguise herself as the correct mom every time. With the right key, and the right look, anyone who saw her come and go would think they were seeing someone else. Which happened twice, remember. Those nosy neighbors didn't see your moms, they saw Aunt Sharon here."

With Aunt Sharon pinned on her side, items were starting to drop out of her coat pockets. The house key she'd used, a pair of gloves, and a notepad. I stooped down and picked up the notepad. Clipped inside it, next to a string of copied-down account numbers and e-mail addresses, was a USB memory stick.

"Downloaded a batch of browser cookies and firewall settings, have you?" I asked, wiping snot off my upper lip with Liz's tissue.

"Never seen that before in my life," snarled Aunt Sharon.

Miss Bennett handed her phone to Oliver while trying to keep hold of the wriggling woman beneath her. "Here, call the police. Then call the school. We'll need to speak to all of your parents."

Once the police had taken charge of Aunt Sharon

and been given the address of where they'd find "Monsieur Jacques," we returned to school in the van. Miss Bennett's entire class gave me a huge cheer, which was nice, and Harry Lovecraft got called into the principal's office, which was even nicer.

As it turned out, the police had been on the trail of Uncle "Jacques" Lovecraft for half a dozen different crimes. Although, I'm sorry to say, impersonating a Frenchman wasn't one of them. Aunt Sharon's USB stick was shown to contain personal details pertaining to seventy-seven local people, and to another two hundred and thirty from other parts of the country.

Unfortunately, that low-down rat Harry Lovecraft got off scot-free. His uncle and aunt denied his involvement, and he denied even knowing his uncle and aunt. In the end, there was no firm evidence against him— the money for those new goodies of his could have come from anywhere—and the principal had to drop the matter.

At the start of class the next day, he glided past me with a sneer so extreme it almost fell off his face. "Don't think I'm going to forget this, Smart," he whispered. "One day, I'll have my revenge. One day."

"Looking forward to it," I said, with a polite smile.

That afternoon, I retreated to my shed and my Thinking Chair. I propped my feet up on my desk, and jotted down some notes for my files while the sun slowly set outside the window.

Case closed.

GOFISH

SIMON CHESHIRE

What's your favorite childhood memory?
Reading, in bed, before going to sleep at night.

As a young person, who did you look up to most?
Spider-Man. No, really, Peter Parker in the '60s and '70s Marvel comics was an object lesson in battling through against the odds. I wanted his courage and determination.

What was your worst subject in school?
Anything sports-related. Still gives me the shudders, even today.

What was your best subject in school?
History and English

What was your first job?
Cleaning offices at 3 AM (when I was a student)

How did you celebrate publishing your first book?
By writing another one

Which of your characters is most like you?
Probably Sam, the main character in *Bottomby*. Saxby
Smart is very much the kid I'd like to have been: He's
quite like me, but he has a self-confidence I never had
at that age.

Are you a morning person or a night owl?
Night owl, definitely. Hate getting up.

What's your idea of the best meal ever?
My wife cooks the most wonderful chocolate and lemon
pudding. Any meal which includes that is OK by me.

Which do you like better: cats or dogs?
Neither, I'm allergic to both. Seriously.

Where do you go for peace and quiet?
I'm not sure I've ever actually found it. . . .

What makes you laugh out loud?
The wide-mouth frog joke. Always makes me smile,
always cheers me up.

Who is your favorite fictional character?
Me

What are you most afraid of?
There are so many things that frighten me senseless, I
wouldn't know what to choose. Bacteria, probably.

What time of year do you like best?
100% summer. Don't like cold, don't like rain. And I live in England. Help.

What's your favorite TV show?
Of all time? *Doctor Who,* 1966–1978.

If you could travel in time, where would you go?
Into the future. I'd love to see how things turn out for the human race!

What do you want readers to remember about your books?
That they made them laugh. And the titles, so they can recommend them.

What would you do if you ever stopped writing?
Spend all day reading

What do you like best about yourself?
I'm still alive.

What is your worst habit?
I'd say immodesty, but to be honest, I'm so close to perfect I don't think that counts.

What do you consider to be your greatest accomplishment?
My children

Where in the world do you feel most at home?
In a world of my own

What do you wish you could do better?
Write

What would your readers be most surprised to learn about you?
I'm good at repairing computers.

QUESTIONS FOR THE ILLUSTRATOR

R. W. ALLEY

What did you want to be when you grew up?

That depends on when the question got asked. In third grade, I wanted to be an astronaut or a clown. In sixth grade, I wanted to make puppets and put on shows. In middle school, I wanted to be a space explorer and make puppets. (I was done with the clown thing.) In high school, I wanted to fit in. In college, I thought I might be an art historian or make puppets and puppet movies. (The astronaut thing turned out to require some engineering skill and a strong stomach. It looked so much easier on TV.) Then one day, drawing a cartoon for the school newspaper, I thought, "Maybe I could do this for money." A wild notion, if you'd seen my drawings then.

I told my parents that I was going to be a lawyer.

When did you realize you wanted to be an illustrator?

The summer after college, I wrote and drew a story for fun. I thought it looked like a children's book, maybe. I showed it to a publisher and they bought it. It appeared that I had a career, or at least a job. The law would have to wait.

What's your first childhood memory?

Hard to tell. I've made up too many stories about what I seem to be thinking in my baby pictures.

What's your most embarrassing childhood memory?
(See above.)

What's your favorite childhood memory?
When it was very quiet on Saturday mornings, I'd sit at a little table in front of a small black-and-white TV and make clay figures and make up stories for them while I watched *Captain Kangaroo, Top Cat,* and *Fireball XL5*.

What was your worst subject in school?
Languages have always confused me.

What was your best subject in school?
History and English. My junior high and high school had no arts programs (visual or performing). It wasn't until college that I took an art class. I wasn't very good at it. I could never finish anything. I just kept doing the same project over and over.

What was your first job?
I sold televisions at a local department store. I was not gifted at sales. And the store is no more. Coincidence? You judge.

How did you celebrate publishing your first book?
I forgot to celebrate. I was in the middle of working on a second book.

Where do you work on your illustrations?
In a very nice room that used to be the garage but now has a tall bookcase with a rolling ladder.

Where do you find inspiration for your illustrations?
Everything around me provokes a visual idea. I love architecture and faces. I am always looking and trying

to remember what I see. A very useful skill for an illustrator.

Are you a morning person or a night owl?
I am a morning and a night person. I find the afternoon the most useless for working. Of course, this may be because I am sleepy.

What's your idea of the best meal ever?
Lobster in a restaurant beside the dock where the boat that earlier in the day hauled in the trap that caught my lobster is tied up.

Which do you like better: cats or dogs?
I like the loud variety of dogs and the quiet elegance of cats.

Where do you go for peace and quiet?
Inside my head

What makes you laugh out loud?
My children, my wife, most Monty Python, and a good fart joke

What's your favorite song?
"Try to Remember" from the musical *The Fantasticks*

Who is your favorite fictional character?
Toad, Ratty, Mole, and Badger from *The Wind in the Willows*

What are you most afraid of?
A bad fart joke

What time of year do you like best?
No time of year. Time of day. Early morning and just before midnight.

What's your favorite TV show?
No favorite. None are that consistent.

If you were stranded on a desert island, who would you want for company?
My wife and children. Although, if we don't get a good cell signal, I'm not so sure about the children.

What's the best advice you have ever received about illustrating?
My advice has come from the drawings of the illustrators/artists I admire most: "Make it simple, make it clear, and don't overwork it."

What do you want readers to remember about your books?
Mostly, that they remember them.

What would you do if you ever stopped illustrating?
Do you know something I don't?

What do you consider to be your greatest accomplishment?
My children and a happy marriage

Where in the world do you feel most at home?
In my home

What do you wish you could do better?
Draw horses. I really stink at drawing horses. Also, shoes. Not so good on shoes.

What would your readers be most surprised to learn about you?
Next to lobster, I think an anchovy pizza is the best meal.

With the help of his thinking chair, his brains, and his two best friends, **Saxby Smart** solves three new cases.

Hone your sleuth skills with Saxby

in the third **Saxby Smart** tale,

THE PIRATE'S BLOOD and Other Case Files.

CHAPTER ONE

It was about seven o'clock on a Tuesday evening in the summer. The sky was the clearest, deepest shade of blue I think I'd ever seen, and the air was motionless and warm. I've just had a look in my dictionary, and the perfect word to describe it is balmy.

So, not exactly the kind of weather or the time of year you'd expect to come across a tale of blood-chilling horror. And yet, that was exactly what I was about to come across.

I was standing outside my garden shed, with a jam jar of red poster paint in one hand and a brush in the other. As readers of my earlier case files will know, I'd been fighting a losing battle with the wooden sign—Saxby Smart: Private Detective—which I kept trying to nail up on the shed door. It kept falling off. I am not good at practical things like that.

It had taken me a surprisingly long time to hit on the simple idea of having a painted sign instead. I guess even brilliant schoolboy detectives like me sometimes miss the obvious, ahem, ahem. Anyway, I'd decided on red lettering against a white rectangle painted directly on the door.

I stood back to admire my handiwork. It said: Saxby Smart: Privat Detective.

"Oh rats," I muttered to myself. I painted in the missing "e." It looked a bit squashed, but it was okay.

"Hi Saxby," came a voice from behind me. I turned to see a boy from my class at school, James Russell, poking his head around the garden gate. He looked as nervous as a kid in his first spelling bee. "I need your help."

I opened the freshly painted shed door and ushered him into my office. "Sorry, just step around the lawnmower," I said. "Watch out for the garden hose, that's it. You sit in my Thinking Chair, I'll sit on the desk. Now then, you have a tale to tell me?"

"It's a tale of blood-chilling horror," he said shakily.

"Excellent," I said. "Begin."

For a moment or two, James cast his eyes around the cluttered interior of the shed. He was known around school as a quiet, serious kid. He had a face that looked like it had been sculpted out of assorted sizes of triangle, and a shock of curly hair that tended to sway as he walked.

"Have you heard of Captain Virgil Blade?" he said.

"Nope," I said. "But I'd love to borrow his name sometime."

"He was a pirate in the seventeenth century," said James. "He commanded a ship that raided merchant vessels all along the French and Spanish coasts. Pirates never lasted long in those waters, because the local navy ships went after them, but Captain Blade outran and outgunned them for ten years. He was the most feared pirate on the seas, and he thought nothing of killing entire crews just to get at a valuable cargo. It's said he had his own grandmother beheaded, just so she couldn't give away his location."

"Nice man," I muttered.

"When he was caught in 1675," said James, "he

swore to gain vengeance from beyond the grave. As he stood on the gallows at Portsmouth dock, he vowed that his ghost would haunt anyone who ever touched his possessions. A lot of artifacts survive to this day. His coat, a hat he wore, there's even a bottle that's supposed to contain some of his blood."

"Oh yuck!" I said. "For real?"

"It was collected from Blade's dead body by his cabin boy. There were those who believed he'd come back from the dead one day. Over the centuries, there have been rumors of strange noises and eerie sights every time his possessions were moved."

"And they've been moved recently?" I said quietly. I was starting to get a cold feeling at the back of my neck.

James nodded. "My dad is curator at the local museum, up in town. A whole load of Virgil Blade's stuff arrived there a couple of weeks ago. And, I swear to you, Saxby, I think his ghost has arrived along with it!"

CHAPTER TWO

For a moment or two, I went as shuddery as Jell-O in an earthquake. Then I leaned forward, my eyes narrowing.

"Tell me more."

"Captain Blade was born just a few miles from here," said James, "which is why our little museum has managed to get all these artifacts on loan. They're normally kept at some huge maritime archive in London. This is the most important exhibition the museum's ever held. It opened a few days ago."

"And it's attracting a lot of visitors?" I said.

James wrinkled his nose. "Well, no, not really. Even my dad admits the museum isn't exactly a major tourist attraction around here."

I remembered the town museum from a school visit a couple of years before. And what I remembered most was it being rather dark, rather drafty, and rather boring.

"So where does the ghost come in?" I said.

"For a start," said James, reaching into his pocket, "there's this." He unfolded a newspaper clipping and handed it to me. Underneath a picture of a woman who'd obviously been told to look unhappy and to pose like a dummy in front of her shop window was:

GHOSTS SCARE LOCAL TRADER

Spooky noises are making life a misery for Mrs Janet Gumm, owner of Nibblies Cheese Shop in Good Street. Mrs Gumm, 49, has heard ghostly sounds for the past two weeks. 'Almost every day, while the shop is open, I hear strange scraping and clanking noises,' she comments. 'It sounds like a spectre rattling its chains and groaning.'

Mrs Gumm claims that the weird sounds are loudest behind the counter of her shop. 'When you stand next to the cellar hatch,' she says, 'if you hush everyone and strain your ears, now and again you can just make it out. This is ruining my trade. I demand that the council take action or reduce my rates bill!'

"That shop backs onto the museum building," said James.

"Well, it's hardly conclusive," I said. "Old central heating pipes can make noises like that."

"I wouldn't have thought anything of it either," said James, "if it hadn't been for . . . what I saw today."

"You . . . saw something?" I said. That cold feeling at the back of my neck was coming back.

James nodded. He was genuinely scared, and his nervousness was starting to make me feel a little jittery too.

"The Captain Blade exhibition is in the museum's main room," said James. "A lot of the most important items—well, the creepiest items, anyway—are in a very large display case that stands against one wall. I take a look at it every day after school. I went over to it this afternoon, as usual. And near the bottom of the glass, over to one side, there is now a handprint. Quite large, certainly a man's."

"On the glass," I said quietly.

James nodded again. "It's very faint, but it's definitely there. And it definitely was not there yesterday. And . . . this handprint is a reddish color."

"Reddish, why?"

"I have a terrible feeling that . . . it's blood."

That cold feeling was starting to turn my neck into an icicle. "Blood?" I said.

"That bottle I told you about?" said James. "The one with Captain Blade's blood in it? That's one of the artifacts in this display case."

"Hang on a minute," I said. "Let's be logical here. Even if that handprint is made in blood, and I don't for a minute suppose it really is, then we still don't have to start talking about ghosts. Think about it. Even a quiet museum like yours is going to have a few visitors each day. Someone has

obviously been looking at the Captain Blade exhibition and touched the glass, leaving a print. You never know, it might even have been left there deliberately, by someone trying to create exactly the spooky effect it's had on you."

James shifted forward in the chair. "You don't understand, Saxby. That handprint is on the inside of the glass. It's been made by something inside the display case."

That cold feeling was now freezing half my spine and turning my nerves into running water.

"It's . . . what?" I whispered.

"Now do you see?" said James. "It's Captain Blade's ghost. It has to be. He's come back to guard his possessions, just like he said he would!"

I took a couple of deep breaths. "Who else knows about this handprint?"

"Nobody," said James. "Just you and me."

"Okaaaaay," I said. I wanted to sound as if I had a definite plan. But I didn't even have a vague and sketchy plan, let alone a definite one!

"I'll come over to the museum after summer school tomorrow," I said. "There's got to be more to this than we're seeing. There's simply got to be. In the meantime, I'll need my Thinking Chair. Saxby Smart is on the case!"